FAMILIAR SPIRITS

SARA CHRISTENE

Copyright © 2020 by Sara Christene

All rights reserved.

No part of this book may be reproduced in any form or by any electronic or mechanical means, including information storage and retrieval systems, without written permission from the author, except for the use of brief quotations in a book review.

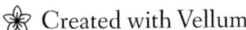 Created with Vellum

CHAPTER ONE

The last of my regulars had finally filtered out of the Toasty Bean cafe. It was 7 PM, an hour after closing time, but no one really paid attention to the hours. I turned the key in the lock, then started walking with a stack of books clutched under one arm. My house was only four blocks away, but that wasn't out of the ordinary in Twilight Hollow, Washington. Everything was four or so blocks away.

I rounded the corner, jingling my keys in time with my low-heeled boots. I took a deep breath, reveling in the first hint of crispness that meant summer was almost over, and autumn was on its way. My curly red hair swirled around me in the breeze.

I passed the bank, and the laundromat, then headed west down Mueller Street.

"Meow!"

I stopped walking, glancing both ways. I could have sworn I heard a cat, but I wasn't used to seeing one on this route.

When no further meows presented themselves, I started walking again, but didn't make it far before the toe of my boot caught on a crack in the sidewalk. The books I had clutched under one arm went flying, and I followed right after them, landing hard on my hands and knees. I nearly screamed at a sudden weight on my back.

Slowly, I craned my neck to look over my shoulder, feeling like I was in a horror movie.

A black cat stood atop my back. "Meow."

I glared at the creature. "Can I help you?"

She, or he, I wasn't sure, hopped down from my back and circled in front of me, sitting down near my fallen books. I was glad it was just a cat seeing my books and not one of my sisters. A natural witch shouldn't need to study witchcraft, but I was pretty sure I was defective.

The cat watched me with amber eyes. It was skinny and a bit mangy with jet black fur.

I pushed myself up, sitting back on my heels. "It looks like you haven't had a meal in a while. Do you want to come home with me?"

"Meow."

"I'll take that as a yes." I gathered my books, then stood and looked down at the cat. "Are you going to let me pick you up?"

"Meow."

I took that as another yes, and knelt beside the cat, scooping it up with my free arm. The cat did not protest, and we started walking.

"You know black cats are supposed to be unlucky," I said as we continued on. "But I think that's just silly superstition. Maybe having a black cat will make me a better witch."

The cat and I both startled at the sound of a falling trashcan around the next corner. I stopped long enough to register what the sound was, then continued on, thinking little of it. That was, until I went around the corner. I saw the fallen trashcan, and beyond that a pair shoes. A pair of shoes still attached to feet, with the toes sticking up skyward.

"Meow?"

I glanced down at the cat, then over to the pair of shoes. It was getting dark. My eyes had to be playing tricks on me. Holding my breath, the cat, and my books, I crept forward. I peered over the trashcan at the owner of the shoes. Neil Howard lay sprawled on his back, dead as a door nail.

I dropped my books as I stumbled back, but managed to maintain my hold on the cat. Fortunately the creature didn't struggle, even though I was careening away like a mad woman. I glanced frantically around the street. I had heard that trashcan fall, and Neil's death was *not* a natural occurrence. I could tell that much by the knife sticking out of his chest.

Keeping my eyes trained on my surroundings, I pulled my cell phone from my back pocket and dialed 911.

Before the woman on the other end could say her spiel, I blurted, "I need to report a murder!"

I followed her instructions and stayed on the line, and the cat stayed calmly in my arms. Eventually the sirens came, and I spotted the flashing lights. In a small town, cops responded fast. It was a perk I'd hoped to never experience.

The two uniformed officers, a man and a woman, barely looked at me and the cat as they rushed over to Neil. One checked his pulse, even though he was clearly dead. Ambulance sirens wailed in the distance.

The male officer walked toward me, while the female stayed with Neil, watching over the corpse like someone might come snatch it away.

The officer who reached me was mid-fifties, salt and pepper hair, a bit of a paunch hanging over his dark blue slacks. "I take it you're Adelaide O'Shea?" At my nod, he continued, "What were you doing when you found the body?" He noticed my books on the ground, and proceeded to stare at them.

I chewed my lip, clutching the cat like it was my favorite stuffed animal. "I was just walking home from work. I heard the trashcan fall, and came around the corner to find Neil."

His bushy brows raised. "Walking home from work with your pet cat?" His tone oozed skepticism. He looked down at my books again.

I felt my cheeks going red. Everyone knew that witchcraft wasn't real. This cop clearly thought I was a nut, walking around with my black cat and spell books. It would serve him right if I hexed him, but I'm not particularly good at hexes. I could always ask my sister, Luna, to do it. She was the queen of hexes.

The ambulance arrived, saving me from answering any further questions for the moment. Along with the ambulance came an unmarked cop car. The officer questioning me looked at the car with a scowl, which deepened as a man stepped out.

The newcomer surveyed the scene quickly, his dark eyes ending up on me. He flashed a badge as he approached. "Logan White, homicide. Did you find the body?"

I snapped my mouth shut, afraid I might start drooling. He was the definition of tall, dark, and handsome. His skin, hair, and features hinted at Native American heritage. He was around six foot, a little on the thin side but definitely in shape. Maybe a runner.

I nodded a little too quickly as the paramedics exited the ambulance and walked toward the body. Though one still checked the pulse, it was clear they knew dead when they saw it.

"Did you see anything else unusual?" the detective asked, drawing my attention back to him.

My brows knit together. "You mean other than the knife sticking out of his chest?" I shook my head. "I heard the trash cans fall before I came around the corner, but I didn't see anyone else around."

He looked me up and down, his eyes first lingering on the cat, then on my fallen books. His eyes lifted back to me. "Give the officer here your details and head home. I'll call you if I have any more questions."

The officer opened his mouth as if to argue, but one look from Detective White made him shut it.

I set the cat down so I could gather up my books. The creature twined around my ankles while I gave the officer my information. With a final look at the body, I scooped up the cat, then hurried home.

Maybe the cat was unlucky after all, but I couldn't bring myself to set it free. We both needed a nice meal and a warm bed, and things would be better in the morning.

Famous last words, or something like that.

CHAPTER TWO

My sister Luna came bursting through my front door with a convenience store bag looped over one arm, and a bottle of wine in the other hand.

I startled, nearly spilling my tea on my white sofa, though I knew Luna was coming. I had asked her for a little bit of moral support, and for some food for my new friend.

She closed the door behind her, then looked at the cat as it came up to inspect her. Though Luna is an inch shorter than my 5'6", she's all curves and has a big presence to boot. If there's anything Luna knew how to do, it was to take up the space she deserved with her deep laughter, too many hugs, and glowing confidence.

She shucked her forest green cardigan to reveal a mustard yellow tee shirt, then knelt down before the cat, tossing her thick auburn hair over her shoulder. All of the O'Shea women have red hair, but Luna's is the darkest. My gingery hue is in the middle, and our youngest sister, Callie, has strawberry blonde.

Luna pawed through her shopping bag, then pulled out a can of cat food. "I come bearing gifts, let's be friends."

"Meow!" The cat went running toward the adjoining kitchen like he knew what he was doing. At least, I was pretty sure he was a he at this point. Someone had gotten him fixed, and I was no expert on cats, but he definitely had boy cat energy.

Luna stood, chuckling to herself, then headed after the cat. She stopped in front of the couch on her way, handing me the bottle of wine. "Be a dear and open that, little sis." She continued on into the kitchen with cat food in hand.

I caught up to find her searching through my cupboard for a dish. Finding one to her liking, she dumped the cat food on it while I poured us each a glass of wine. Luna put the little plate she'd found on the floor in front of the cat, and I handed her a glass.

Wine in hand, she crossed her arms and leaned her butt against the counter. Her chocolate brown eyes looked me over. "So Neil Howard, huh? I wonder who would want to kill him."

I took a long swill of my wine, then leaned against

the other counter across from her. "You seem pretty calm knowing your sister just found a murder victim. The killer could still be in the neighborhood."

She shrugged one shoulder. "We're witches, Addy, a killer wouldn't dare come for us."

I pursed my lips. What she meant was, a killer wouldn't dare come for *her*. Everyone in town knew that if you crossed Luna, you would have some serious bad luck. Folk whispered rumors that we were witches, though most just took it as superstition. Even so, everyone knew that you didn't step on sidewalk cracks, you didn't say Bloody Mary to your mirror at night, and you didn't mess with Luna O'Shea.

Thinking of another superstition, I looked down at my new black cat just as he licked the last remnants from his dish. "Do you think he has an owner? He seems pretty skinny."

Luna sipped her wine and watched the cat. "I'd say if he had an owner, it was a long time ago. He needs a steady diet and a good bath." Her eyes flicked up to me. "You're going to keep him, aren't you? It's bad luck to turn away a cat when it has already chosen you."

I looked down at the cat in question, now inspecting my small dining table overlooking my backyard window. "I highly doubt this creature is a witch's familiar."

She lifted her shoulder in another half-shrug. "Well you've never had a familiar, so how would you know?"

I frowned. Just another way I was defective. Luna was good with hexes and divination, Callie was into matchmaking and love potions, but me? All I was good for was brewing coffee and tea that brought people a cozy happy feeling. While my magic had helped me build a successful business, it wasn't exactly useful in any other sense.

"I don't think he's my familiar," I decided. "But if I can't find his owner, if he even has one, I'll keep him. At least as long as he wants to stay."

Luna sat her empty wine glass on the counter, then stood up straight, stretching her arms over her head with a yawn. "So what are you going to name him?"

I looked down at the cat, who blinked up at me with deep yellow eyes. "I think I'll name him Spooky."

"Spooky? What kind of name is that for a cat?"

I smiled down at Spooky. "Well he scared me half to death when we met, and shortly after that we found a murder victim. And he's a black cat with yellow eyes. I think Spooky is pretty fitting."

Luna turned to fill herself another glass of wine. "Whatever you say, Addy." She turned back to me and drained half her glass in one swill. "Let's make some dinner. If I'm going to stay the night to keep you safe, then you better feed me."

I crossed my arms and raised my brows. "Don't you

want to know anything more about the murder? Aren't you curious?"

She gave me her best secretive smile. "Sure I'm curious, but I'm going to find out eventually. After all, you're going to be the one to solve it."

I nearly dropped my glass. Luna only had visions occasionally, but they always came true.

Spooky hopped up on the counter and nuzzled my arm until I pet him. I shook my head, looking at the cat. "I take it back. You are *entirely* unlucky."

CHAPTER THREE

Spooky wound around my ankles the next morning as I started the first orders at the cafe. My four regulars had appeared at once, anxious to know details on Neil's murder. In small towns, word traveled unbelievably fast.

Francis and Elmer Brookes were always here at this hour, but Francis made her interest abundantly clear by marching up to the counter and demanding a full recount of events.

"The usual, Francis?" I asked, already measuring out the ground beans for her coffee.

She moved her ample figure closer to the counter, smoothing a stray hair back into her tight gray bun. She had to be nearly eighty, but looked younger and was sharp as a tack. She had the same twinkle in her eyes that she got whenever I found a new book for her to read. "I heard Neil was cut up into pieces," she whispered conspiratorially.

Francis' husband, Elmer, put a hand on her shoulder. He was as tall and thin as she was short and plump. "We'll both have the usual, thanks Addy."

Richie Garcia sat at his regular spot back by the rows of bookshelves taking up the left side of the cafe. "And we'll all take the story, if you don't mind!" he called out. Richie was in his early twenties and considered himself a poet, though his preferred style of dress reminded me of James Dean. His strong Hispanic features were emphasized by his slicked back black hair.

Normally Richie was quiet, but he was used to being around Elmer and Francis, and the only other person in the cafe was Sophie Turner.

"Earl Grey?" I asked Richie, ignoring yet another demand for the murder story.

"You know it."

I looked to Sophie, sitting at the table next to Richie's, twirling the end of her blonde ponytail. Sophie was painfully shy, and I had a feeling she only came into the cafe to see Richie. "Peppermint latte?" I asked her.

She nodded gratefully, pleased that I didn't make her speak.

Finished with the first two orders, I handed the Brookes their coffees.

Francis took her cup, still staring at me intently.

I rolled my eyes. "I'll tell you what little I know, just give me a minute."

This seemed to satisfy her, and she and Elmer went to sit at Richie's table.

Spooky went to inspect the bookshelves as I finished up the other two orders, then delivered them myself, taking the extra seat at Sophie's table. In the mornings, this was where all the regulars sat. In the evenings, everyone moved to the charcoal gray microfiber couches making up a nice cozy corner opposite the bookshelves. The used books were all for sale, but I didn't mind if customers read them while they sat and drank their coffee.

"Where did the cat come from?" Sophie asked in her soft voice.

"I don't like cats," Francis grumbled.

I counted to ten in my head. Francis could be a handful, but she meant well, and Elmer was nothing but a big teddy bear.

"Spooky found me on my walk home yesterday," I told Sophie. "It seems I am his chosen one."

Her smile broadened. I had been trying for a while to get Sophie to come out of her shell.

"*Details*, Addy," Richie interrupted. "I'm dying over here."

He leaned back in his seat, tugging his leather jacket straight. His Earl Grey sat steaming on the counter. He most certainly did not appear to be dying, but I put him out of his misery anyway.

"There's not much to tell. I was walking home, I heard a crash, and when I came around the corner I found Neil with a knife in his chest."

Francis and Elmer's eyes widened.

"So he really was knifed to death?" Elmer asked.

"Seems that way. I called the cops, gave my statement, and went home."

Richie had leaned forward, gripping his tea in both hands. "They'll question you some more. Cops always have more questions."

I assumed he was speaking from the experience of reading a book rather than experience with actual cops. I knew his mom, and Richie would no longer be among the living if he had experience with actual cops.

I shrugged. "I don't know what else I would be able to tell them."

Luna's words came to mind about me solving the murder, but she had to be wrong. I hardly even knew Neil Howard.

The door jingled, and we all looked that way. The detective, Logan White, stepped inside.

I stood, wiping my hands on my jeans. Looking at his expensive suit, I suddenly felt under-dressed in my pumpkin orange sweater. It didn't look good with my hair, but I loved the color so I wore it anyway.

"A word, Ms. O'Shea?"

"Told you," Richie muttered under his breath.

I wove my way through the tables, heading back toward the counter.

"In private," Logan added.

I gave him a suspicious look, but I wasn't about to argue with a detective. "We can go back to the office." I looked to Richie. "Keep an eye on the counter, would you?"

He nodded, his eyes glittering with excitement.

What I referred to as an office was actually a maintenance closet just big enough to fit a small desk and two chairs. Once we were closed inside, I regretted the decision to bring him back. It was way too quiet. *Awkward.*

We both sat, and I laced my fingers on top of the desk and tried to look professional. "What can I help you with, detective?"

He leaned back in the small plastic chair. "How well did you know Neil Howard?"

I felt my shoulders hunching, and forced them to straighten. I tucked a loose curl behind my ear "Not well at all. I don't think I even spoke to him more than a handful of times. He never came into the cafe."

So this is what it means to have a good cop face, I thought as Logan watched me. I had no idea what he was thinking, or trying to imply.

He pulled a plastic bag out of his blazer pocket, then

slid it across the desk. There was a piece of paper inside. "Is that your handwriting?"

I looked down at the paper, then lifted my brows. "No, but that's my phone number."

"Yes," he said, "the same number you left with the officer after finding the body. We found that piece of paper in Neil's back pocket. Any idea what it was doing there?"

I gave him wide eyes. "I have absolutely no idea, detective."

"When was the last time you spoke to Mr. Howard?"

I furrowed my brow as the first hint of anger stiffened my spine. "What exactly are you trying to imply?"

He leaned forward. "You found the body. You claimed to barely know him, yet he had your phone number in his pocket. Seems a little strange."

I tilted my head with a smile. "Well now, if we were close, as you're implying, I don't see why he'd need to have my phone number written down. Wouldn't he have it memorized?"

The corner of his lip ticked up. "Do you always walk home an hour after closing time?"

I refused to let my smile fall. He had obviously done his research on me. "My regulars like to stay late. Richie and Sophie left here at the same time I did last night. You can march right on out and ask them if you don't believe me."

His laughter transformed his face from handsome, intimidating model, to just a regular guy. "You've made your point, Ms. O'Shea. But you should know, you are currently our only lead."

"Call me Addy, and if that's the case, you must not be very good at your job."

He laughed again. He might be accusing me of murder, but at least he had a sense of humor.

He stood, then withdrew a card from his coat pocket and slid it across the desk. "Call me if you think of anything, Addy, and don't leave town."

I waited inside my office after he left. Once the door was shut, I buried my face in my hands. Last night, when Luna said that I would be solving the case, I couldn't imagine a reason why.

Now, being the prime suspect was a pretty good reason.

CHAPTER FOUR

I avoided everyone's questions for the rest of the morning. I most certainly did not need it spread around that I was the sole suspect in a murder investigation. At noon Evie Taylor, my only employee, came in for her shift, her eight year old daughter in tow.

Evie's kinky curls frothed around her trim jaw, barely skimming the shoulders of her emerald green blouse, which contrasted nicely with her rich brown skin. She smiled after her daughter, Sedona, as she ran for the bookshelves.

"Long day?" Evie asked as she approached the counter.

I wrinkled my nose. "Do I look that bad?"

"You look that stressed. I heard about Neil."

I glanced past her to the few customers, but none were paying attention. The regulars had long since departed, leaving me in peace. I was saved from further explanation as Spooky came around the corner and looked up at Evie.

"Who is this?" she asked, kneeling down to pet the cat.

I leaned across the counter. "That's Spooky. I was hoping you could watch over things here so I can take him to the vet."

Finished petting Spooky, she stood and wiped her hand on her pants. "Maybe a trip to the groomer is in order too. I have things covered here. Marcus will be by to pick up Sedona at two."

I grabbed my purse from behind the counter and swung it over my shoulder. "You're the best. If anyone asks you about the murder, just say you don't know anything."

She lifted a brow. "Addy, I *don't* know anything."

I walked around the counter and scooped up Spooky. "I'll fill you in on the details later. If a handsome detective happens to come in, tell him I said to screw off."

Evie's chocolate brown eyes widened. "Do you really want me to do that?"

I sighed. "No, but maybe punish him with decaf if he tries to order a coffee."

I waved to Evie and the few customers, then headed out the door and started walking.

A new vet clinic had opened on the other side of

town the previous year, but I hadn't had a reason to stop in since I didn't have a pet until now. I had seen the vet around town a few times, but it didn't seem he was a coffee or tea drinker. Or else he went somewhere else.

I glanced at the clouds overhead, threatening rain, and debated walking home to get my car, but thought better of it. When you lived your entire life in Washington state, you learned to not worry about a little bit of rain.

I looked down at Spooky in my arms. "If I set you down, will you follow me?"

"Meow."

I took a chance and set the cat down. The only roads through town had a speed limit of twenty-five miles per hour, we should be all right for now, though I'd probably need to pick up a carrier eventually.

Spooky twined around my ankles, then stuck close as I started walking. A few people glanced my way as we walked, but I paid them little mind. I was used to the glancing, and most likely no one was surprised that the red-haired witch now had a black cat.

I tipped an imaginary hat toward Maura Wimbledon, the old librarian, as she walked past us in the other direction. "You just let me know when you want another order of pastries," she called after me.

"Thanks, Maura," I said with a wave, trying not to be humiliated.

I'd been running the cafe for three years now, you'd think I would have learned to bake, but everything I made turned out awful. I couldn't seem to put the same magic into my food that I did into my coffee and tea.

Eventually we reached the vet's office, and I stood out on the sidewalk, realizing I probably should have made an appointment. Spooky sat next to my left boot, staring at the door with me.

"Are you going inside, are you just trying to open the door with your mind?" a voice said from behind me.

I turned to find the veterinarian himself, minus his white lab coat, smiling down at me. I guessed he was around 5'11". His light brown hair was cut into one of those tousled styles that looked effortless, but probably took all morning. Though his easy smile and no fuss flannel and jeans almost made me reconsider the hair. Maybe it did just look that good naturally. I placed him around his late thirties, maybe just a year or two older than me.

"Well I walked all the way down here, then I realized I hadn't made an appointment."

He laughed. "You're in luck, I just finished up my lunch break a little early and my next appointment isn't until one."

I smiled back, then scooped Spooky up from the sidewalk. "And here I was starting to think that this cat was unlucky."

We headed toward the door, and the vet held it open for me.

I took a quick look around inside. It was a small space, but how much space did you really need in such a small town? There was a receptionist desk with a little card that said *out to lunch*.

He grabbed his white coat from a hook on the wall. "You can head on back, Ms . . ." he hesitated.

"Call me Addy." I walked in the direction he pointed down the only hall.

"First room, Addy, and I'm Max by the way. I'll just grab your paperwork real quick."

Max the vet retrieved a clipboard, then followed me back. He had me set Spooky on the table so he could look him over while I filled out the paperwork. I told him he was a stray, but I intended to keep him.

"Well," Max said, "he seems healthy. I can give him his vaccinations and he should be good to go." He pet Spooky, who obliged by rubbing his face against his hand.

Max left us alone to fetch the vaccinations, and I did some light snooping while he was gone. A framed degree on the wall told me his last name, Howard. It was a common last name, but might he be related to Neil?

He returned and gave Spooky his shots. The cat wailed like a banshee, then hissed at Max when he tried to come near him again.

Max stepped back, hands raised in surrender. "All right, we're done. Calm down." He looked up to me. "We can settle your tab at the front. I'll let *you* carry the cat."

Grinning, I picked up Spooky, who was happy to ride halfway up my shoulder with my left arm curled around his bottom. It seemed the blame for the needles went all on Max.

I followed Max through the doorway with the cat watching everything behind us as I tried to figure out how to ask him about Neil.

The price he gave me at the front desk seemed a little low, but I wasn't about to argue. He looked over the paperwork I had filled out, typing my information into the computer. A moment later, the printer came to life, spitting out Spooky's new vaccination records.

Max took another glance at the paperwork, then looked up to me with the clipboard in one hand. "You wouldn't happen to be the Adelaide who found Neil, would you?"

My eyes widened and my arm reflexively tightened around the cat. Spooky struggled until I put him down on the ground. "Honestly, I was just about to ask if you knew him. I saw your last name on your degree."

"He was my cousin," he explained. "We weren't close." He shrugged. "But I'd still kind of like to know what happened to him."

"Understandable," I said, handing him my credit

card. "But I don't know what I can tell you that you don't already know. I found the body, but as of yet the police don't have any meaningful suspects." It wasn't quite a lie. I wasn't a *meaningful* suspect.

Seeing as the cute vet was my only lead, I continued, "Can you think of anyone who would want to hurt Neil?"

He gave me a sad smile as he handed me back my card, receipt, and vaccination certificate. "Plenty of folk, unfortunately. He was recently separated from his wife, and according to her he owed a few people money."

I was glad I asked. The wife seemed like a good place to start.

"Well Max," I held out my hand. "It was a pleasure doing business with you. If you ever find yourself in need of a tea or coffee, come by the Toasty Bean."

His smile was wide enough that I thought he might be flirting with me. "I'll do that, Addy. I'll see you around."

I picked up Spooky, then left with a wave. First, I needed to take Spooky to the groomer and get back to the cafe. After that, I'd figure out where Neil's estranged wife could be found, and in the morning I'd pay her a visit.

I smiled down at Spooky as we walked. "I guess we're detectives now, my friend. Let's see if we can't drum us up a murderer."

CHAPTER FIVE

It was dark by the time I left the cafe, clutching a freshly laundered Spooky to my chest like a security blanket. All was quiet as we hit Mueller Street.

"As long as I don't find another dead body, I'll be good," I muttered.

I had a bag looped over one elbow with more cat food and ingredients for cat treats. I didn't really want to try making the cat treats, but one of my customers had insisted the recipe was fool proof, and I was simply a bad cat mom if I didn't try it.

I would most certainly not be a bad cat mom, so I guess I had to bake the treats.

Wind scented with dying leaves gusted, blowing my curly hair back from my face and sending goosebumps up my arms beneath my sweater and coat. I had never been afraid of walking home at night, but knowing there was a murderer lurking about had me on edge.

A prickle of magic crept up my spine. It was the type of sensation like recognizing an old, nostalgic scent that you can't quite place. It was overwhelming and you knew it was important, but that was it.

I stopped walking, glancing around the dark street. Most of the homes had lights on inside. If I needed help, I could always run and knock on someone's door.

"Meow?" Spooky questioned.

I gave him a light squeeze. "Nothing, it's nothing."

Shaking my head at my own foolishness, I started walking again. Soon we'd be back home, safe behind a locked door, or so I kept telling myself as I hurried along.

We were almost halfway home when Spooky started hissing and spitting. He let out a low, threatening wail.

I stopped walking and looked down at him in my arms, worried that he'd somehow gotten hurt, but his eyes were trained on the narrow alleyway to my right.

I looked that way, but couldn't see much in the darkness.

Run, a voice shot through my mind.

I didn't question where the voice came from. I could sense that weird prickling magic again. I ran like my life depended on it, and maybe it did.

I reached my front door huffing and puffing, fumbling the keys out of my coat pocket. I must have glanced over my shoulder twenty times before getting it unlocked. We hurried inside and I let Spooky down to the floor so I could slam the door shut and lock it.

I flipped on the light switch next to me, then braced my back against the door, panting.

Spooky sat on the wood floor in front of me, looking up. I glanced over my white couch, matching chairs, and small TV.

I laughed. "Well that was ridiculous. I never even heard footsteps. It's not like someone was chasing us."

Spooky watched me for a moment, then turned and walked toward the kitchen.

"Yeah, I'm hungry too," I agreed.

My cell phone rang in my pocket as I headed toward the kitchen. I switched my bag of cat goods to the other arm and answered it.

"Are you safe?" Luna's voice came through the other end.

I set my shopping bag on the kitchen counter. "Of course I'm safe, why wouldn't I be?"

"I had a vision of someone or something chasing you. It was too dark. I couldn't see what it was."

My mouth went dry. "Well that's unsettling." I told her about my frantic run home.

"I am out at mom's, but I'm going to send Callie over to stay with you."

I scowled. "I don't need my younger sister to protect me. I am safe at home behind locked doors."

"I have a feeling whatever this thing is, it doesn't care about locked doors. I'm calling Callie."

Her words made me shiver. I looked across the kitchen to the dark window glass. "Okay, send her over. But next time you get a vision, try to make it a little more clear."

We hung up. I crossed my arms and leaned against the counter in my small kitchen as I looked down at Spooky. "Did you sense something out there? Is that why you started hissing?"

Spooky blinked amber eyes at me.

"You're probably just hungry," I sighed.

I opened a can for him, removed my coat, then set to making the treats. I'd wait on my own dinner until Callie arrived, just in case she was hungry too.

The recipe wasn't too difficult, and it took my mind off of Luna's vision. I even shaped the treats into little fish.

Spooky watched me as I put them in the oven.

"Don't get your hopes up," I said. "Everyone knows I'm a terrible baker."

The doorbell rang as I shut the oven. I hurried out of the kitchen, taking the time to look through the peephole before unlocking the door. Callie stood outside with takeout bags slung over both arms. She had on a cropped leather jacket, covering most of her tattoos.

I unlocked and opened the door, inviting her inside.

I eyed her takeout bags as she walked past in a cloud of lavender essential oil. "Luna tells you something dark was chasing me and you take the time to stop for takeout?"

She turned to me, flipping her strawberry blonde curls over her shoulder. "She didn't see any more danger for you, I'm only here as a precaution, so we might as well have food. I'm not expecting *you* to make anything for me."

"My cooking is not that bad," I grumbled as she headed toward the kitchen.

I followed her in, watching her set the bags on the counter before pulling out the little takeout boxes. The smell of cheap, delicious Chinese food filled the kitchen.

Callie glanced over her shoulder at the oven, her light brown eyes skeptical. "Wait, are you actually baking?" She abandoned the takeout, bending her tall, wiry frame to peer through the glass oven door.

"Just some treats for Spooky," I explained. "One of my customers gave me a recipe."

She straightened. "And where is the illustrious Spooky? I'd like to meet him before he drops dead from eating your baking."

As if knowing he'd been summoned, Spooky strutted

back into the kitchen, then approached to sniff Callie's black boots.

She crouched down and stroked a hand down his back. "Ooh, he is spooky. A proper black spooky cat." Still petting the cat, she looked up to me. "Do you think he's your familiar? Have you noticed any improvements in your magic?"

"He's just a cat," I said, moving to the oven. The treats were only supposed to bake a few minutes.

I opened the oven door, then grabbed the fork I'd left out on the countertop to poke one of the treats. Nice and crunchy. I pulled them out of the oven and set them on the stove.

Callie hovered over my shoulder. "You know, those don't look half bad." She snatched one from the hot pan, then proceeded to toss it back-and-forth between her hands until it cooled.

I turned with my hands on my hips. "Those are cat treats. You shouldn't eat one."

She shrugged. "I'm sure it's fine."

She lifted the little crunchy fish up to her mouth and took a bite, then chewed thoughtfully.

"Well?" I asked, feeling a little anxious about the results.

"Fishy." She tilted her head and took another bite. She chewed and swallowed. "But not half bad."

I lifted my brows, totally shocked.

Callie took another treat from the pan, cooled it in her hands, then offered it to Spooky.

He sniffed it for a moment, then grabbed it in his mouth and started crunching it.

I watched him with my jaw agape. Had I actually managed to bake something that wasn't repulsive?

"Maybe he really is your familiar," Callie said as she turned back to the Chinese food. "We already know your magic shows up in your tea and coffee. Maybe now it can finally show up in your food."

She said it so casually, not realizing what her words meant to me. I picked Spooky up and gave him a squeeze. Maybe I really did finally have a familiar. Maybe I wasn't a totally defective witch after all.

The feeling of being chased came back to me, and of that dark, prickling magic.

It occurred to me, suddenly, that maybe being a real witch wasn't all it was cracked up to be.

CHAPTER SIX

I never thought I would be the type of witch to wake up early to bake, yet here I was, at 6 AM, two cups of coffee in, pulling a pan of freshly baked chocolate chip cookies out of the oven. Evie was going to open the cafe for me so I could visit Neil's estranged wife, Sasha. Of course, as far as Evie knew, I was just taking the morning off to spend time with my sister, which wasn't entirely off.

The sister in question shuffled into the kitchen just as I set the pan on the stovetop. She pushed her hair out of her face, fluffy from sleep, and narrowed her eyes at the cookies.

Her tattooed arms were bare this morning in a white tank top paired with plaid flannel pajama pants.

She leaned forward over the cookies and took a deep inhale. "Well, they smell like cookies."

I lifted my chin, proud of my handiwork. I wasn't sure how they would taste, but they definitely looked better than anything I'd ever made. "There's enough for breakfast. We need to try them before I bring any to Sasha."

Callie lifted a brow as she straightened. We had discussed questioning Sasha the previous night, and she had agreed to come with me since she did Sasha's taxes every year. They were at least acquaintances. "You're hoping your cookies will work a little magic on her, aren't you?"

I shrugged. "I don't have high hopes, but even if they can put her a bit at ease, she might tell us more than she would have otherwise."

She grinned as she snatched a cookie off the hot pan. "Devious. I like it." She bit into the cookie and chewed. Her eyes went wide. "Addy, this is actually good!"

I blinked at her for a moment, then lifted a cookie and had to toss it from hand to hand. Callie made it look like it wasn't that hot. Once the cookie was cool enough, and I had melted chocolate all over my palms, I took a bite.

I chewed slowly, ready for the worst. Perfectly sweetened cookie crumbles swished around in my mouth, with just enough cinnamon to bring out the bittersweet chocolate. By the gods, I had made a damn good cookie.

Callie stole another and ate it in two bites. "You

know what," she said with her mouth half-full, "I am feeling pretty safe and cozy. Just like I feel when I drink a cup of your coffee."

We both looked to the opposite counter where Spooky sat watching us.

"That damn cat is your familiar, Addy. You finally have one."

I grinned. If the cat treats didn't prove it, the cookies most certainly did. "Get dressed. We need to deliver some cookies to a widow."

Callie looked me up and down, starting with my low-heeled brown boots and jeans, and ending with my chunky forest green sweater. "You know, now that you're a proper witch, you should start dressing the part."

She snatched another cookie and sauntered out of the kitchen.

I was too excited to care about her insulting my wardrobe. I poured myself a fresh cup of coffee then went to the opposite counter where Spooky still sat.

I stroked my hand across his clean, silky fur. "You know, some familiars can speak into their witches' minds. Do you feel like having a chat?"

"Meow?"

I patted Spooky's head. "I didn't think so, but we can keep trying."

I was in the mood to celebrate, so I decided to indulge in another cookie. I smiled as the sweetness lifted my spirits, and the chocolate melted in my mouth. Today was going to be a good day.

TODAY WAS MOST CERTAINLY NOT a good day. We pulled up to Sasha's house to find an unmarked police car outside. We debated leaving, then Logan walked out the front door and saw us.

"Crap," I muttered, my hands clenching the steering wheel. I tilted my chin down, bringing my hair forward to hide my face.

Callie sat in the passenger seat with the covered tray of cookies in her lap. She was watching Logan with obvious appreciation. "Oh my, is that the detective you mentioned? He's staring at us."

"That's him," I grumbled. I undid my seatbelt, took my keys, and got out of the car just as Logan was reaching the sidewalk.

He smoothed a hand through his short, dark hair. "Ms. O'Shea, might I ask what you're doing here?"

Callie got out of the car with the tray of cookies in hand, then shut the door with her hip. She had put her leather jacket back on over the white tank top, and the flannel bottoms had been exchanged for torn jeans. "We're here to visit our grieving friend, not that it's any of your concern."

I was glad she'd spoken, because I was finding myself a little tongue-tied.

Logan looked back and forth between the two of us, ending on Callie. "Another Ms. O'Shea, I presume?"

"Callie," she said, bracing the tray against her side to extend her right hand.

I gritted my teeth as they shook hands. All Callie needed was a touch and she would start trying to set that person up with any romantic match she could find. She could read other things about a person too, but she was mostly interested in romance.

Logan's brow lowered as he took his hand back, almost like he could sense Callie's magic, though that wasn't possible.

He turned his attention back to me. "I was thinking I'd come by your cafe again today. Everyone I talk to keeps telling me I need to try the coffee."

I smiled and nodded, though inside I thought, *you're getting decaf.* "I'll be going there after we visit Sasha."

"I'll see you there then." He retreated to his car, leaving me alone with my sister.

She watched him drive away, then looked to me with a mischievous smile. "He's cute. Why do you hate him?"

I crossed my arms. "He accused me of *murder.*"

She rolled her eyes. "He's just doing his job." She started walking toward the door before I could argue.

The door opened before we could reach it. Sasha

must have been watching Logan out the window as he left.

She glanced at both of us, then opened the door wide. Her blonde hair lay pin straight, framing her wide face. She was in her mid-forties, a few years younger than Neil had been. She owned a small jewelry boutique the next town over, which I only knew because Callie did her taxes, which according to my sister, were always separate from Neil's.

She glanced at the tray of cookies in Callie's hands. "I see you heard about Neil." Her voice had the telltale rasp of a lifelong smoker.

Callie extended the cookies. "I wanted to make sure you were all right. I know you and Neil were at odds, but he was still` your husband."

Sasha narrowed her blue eyes at me. "I heard you found his body."

I swallowed the sudden lump in my throat. Of course she knew. I should have been prepared for it. I put on my best sympathetic smile. "Yes I did, unfortunately. I'm sorry for your loss."

She didn't say anything about him having my phone number in his pocket, so the police must be keeping that part secret. For that I was eternally grateful. I did *not* want to try explaining to this woman why her estranged husband had my number.

Sasha looked back and forth between the two of us as

we waited patiently. Her jaw stiffened, but she stepped back. "Won't you both come inside? I'll make us some coffee to go with the cookies."

Callie and I locked gazes as she turned her back. Step one achieved.

Sasha led us into her small, clean home. According to Callie, this was where Sasha and Neil had lived when they were still together. When they split up, Sasha took the house, and Callie's knowledge of the details ended there. The home was meticulously neat and organized, no whiff of cigarette smoke. She had either quit, or smoked outside.

Soon enough we were sitting in Sasha's breakfast nook, sipping atrocious coffee and preparing to eat my cookies.

I found myself staring too hard as Sasha lifted one to her lips.

She hesitated, lowering the cookie. "Is something wrong?"

I startled and didn't have to fake a blush. "Sorry, it's a new recipe. I'm hoping to sell them at my cafe, so I was anxious to see if you liked them."

She still seemed wary, but she took a bite and chewed. "A little dry," she said after swallowing.

A bit of fire flared in my gut, but on the outside I smiled. "Oh well, I guess I need to work on the recipe a bit more then."

Despite her words, Sasha finished her cookie and took another one. Like magic, her petite shoulders relaxed, and she slumped a little further down in her seat.

Callie, sitting next to Sasha, gave me a little wink.

I leaned forward across the small rectangular table. "Sasha, I hope you don't mind me asking, but do you know why anyone would want to hurt Neil? I find myself a little scared after finding him."

She finished a third cookie then dusted her hands. "You mean was it a random killing like a serial killer, or premeditated?"

I nodded encouragingly. "Something like that."

She glanced at Callie, back to me, then sighed. "To tell you the truth, girls, a better question would be who *didn't* want to hurt him. Neil owed a lot of people money, including his dad and brother. I just finished explaining as much to the detective." She looked down at her coffee. "Neil may have been a scoundrel, but I didn't want him dead."

Reading between the lines I could see that Logan had accused her of murder too. I reached across the table and took her hand. "Of course you didn't. No one thinks that."

She batted a tear with her free hand, and I realized I really didn't think that. She was either an excellent actress, or genuinely distraught. For now, Sasha was one suspect I'd be crossing off my list.

She seemed to settle herself, and looked up with glistening eyes. "The police should really be questioning Blake Monroe."

Callie leaned forward with her elbows on the table. "The guy who owns the pawn shop?"

Sasha pulled her hand away to clutch her coffee cup with both hands. "He lost a lot of money in one of Neil's schemes. Neil was never able to pay him back."

"One of his schemes?" I asked.

"Neil always had something in the works. Said he wasn't meant to be a mechanic the rest of his life. He nearly lost our house before I kicked him out. Without his father's help, I'd be destitute." She looked at the tray of cookies, then subtly snatched another.

"Neil's dad bailed him out?" Callie asked.

Sasha's eyes widened. "Oh no, Ike knew better than to give his son money again. It would be like throwing cash into a river. Once I kicked Neil out, Ike helped me save the house."

I tried to keep all the information straight in my head. "That was kind of him."

She shrugged. "I think he felt bad that his son was such a scoundrel. I found lipstick on his collar on more than one occasion. Ike knew about it."

My eyebrows raised. If Neil had been seeing another

woman, that might mean another suspect. "Do you have any idea who it was?"

She shook her head. "By that time I didn't really care to find out." She took a deep breath. "I'm sorry ladies, I think I could use some time alone."

We both stood. I felt a little bad for grilling her, making her relive these painful memories once again.

"Thanks for having us," I said. "If you ever find yourself in need of a comforting cup of tea, come on by the cafe, my treat."

She walked us both to the door, shutting it a little too quickly behind us. I had a feeling she hadn't meant to share so much, but I was glad she did. We now had two more suspects, though we only knew one name.

Blake Monroe. He had come into the cafe on occasion. I might just have to stop by the pawn shop to deliver his favorite drink.

CHAPTER SEVEN

After dropping Callie off and checking on Spooky at home, I walked past the Golden Dollar Pawn Shop. I frowned at the sign taped between the glass and the iron bars on the inside of the door, *Closed until further notice.*

A bit odd that someone who had recent business dealings with Neil would skip town just after his murder. I'd have to ask around and see if anyone knew where Blake ran off to.

With nothing else to do, I headed toward the cafe. I knew Evie wouldn't mind me relieving her a few minutes early. It was a Monday, so she could have some time to herself before Sedona got off school.

In a few minutes I was at the cafe. I opened the door to find a few customers seated here and there, including Francis and Elmer. Max, the cute vet, stood at the counter. He turned at the jingle of the bells attached to the door.

"Ah, there she is," Evie said from behind the counter.

I waved to Elmer and Francis on my way in, then stopped beside Max.

I took in his red flannel shirt and jeans. They looked nice with his short stubble and warm brown eyes. "Day off?"

"I was hoping to try your famous coffee."

Evie was watching us with a little bit too much excitement. Callie might be the self-proclaimed matchmaker of Twilight Hollow, but Evie was a close second.

"Any preference?" I asked, shooting Evie a quick glare.

The corner of Max's mouth ticked up. "I'll take whatever you suggest."

I walked around the counter, giving Evie a meaningful look behind Max's back. "Coming right up."

I set to work on Max's drink while he went to find a table.

Evie hovered near my shoulder with her back to the rest of the cafe. "I see your cat must've made an impression on him," she giggled. Her dark eyes sparkled.

I turned up the milk steamer to drown out her words. "I told him he should come by," I said through gritted teeth. "No big deal. Just a new customer."

She grinned. "Whatever you say, Addy." She breezed

passed me to grab her purse. "Mind if I cut out a little early?"

"Oh, I insist," I said with a laugh.

I finished up Max's drink as Evie walked out the door. Evie might have been set on romance, but I was interested in learning more about Neil.

I walked around the counter to Max's table, carefully balancing the full cup. I slid it in front of him. "Double cinnamon cappuccino. My favorite."

He lifted the cup and gave me a charming smile. "Do you have time to sit?"

I pulled out a chair, tugging the braid I'd put my hair in before work over my shoulder. "I've got a few minutes. It's usually slow this time of day. Plus I have a few questions I want to ask you."

He lifted his brows and leaned back in his seat. "Go on."

"I was wondering if you knew if Neil was seeing someone other than Sasha."

His smile wilted just a bit around the edges. "Well I wouldn't be surprised. He was the type to do something like that. But like I said, we weren't really close."

"What about his father, Ike?" I pressed, leaning forward. "Do you think he would've known if Neil was seeing someone?"

His brows raised a little further. "If I didn't know any better, I'd say you were trying to solve Neil's murder."

"I'm not going to lie, I'm curious." I gestured to his cup. "Your coffee is going to get cold."

He pulled his cup close, but didn't drink. "Oh I don't distract that easily. Why are you so interested in Neil? I know you found the body and all, but isn't solving the murder a job for the police?"

I sighed. Maybe honesty would get me a little further. "All right, fine. The detective on the case accused me of having something to do with the murder. I'd like to clear my name."

If he was surprised, he didn't show it. He smiled and took a sip of his coffee. His shoulders instantly relaxed. "I can see why this is your favorite."

I frowned. "Are you avoiding my questions?"

He took another sip of his coffee. "No, I'll answer them, but under one condition."

I narrowed my eyes. "Go on."

"Let me help. I'll give you any information I have, and in return you'll be up front with me."

I furrowed my brow. "You want to help me solve your cousin's murder?"

"Yep. I may not have liked Neil, but he was still family, and Ike is a good man. He deserves to know what happened to his son."

I considered him for a moment, wondering if he was pulling my leg. "I thought you said solving murders was a job for the police."

He shrugged. "It is, but I have a sneaking suspicion you might learn more than Detective White."

"You met him?" I asked.

"He's been questioning everyone who knew Neil. I don't think he has any real leads to go on yet." He leaned forward and lowered his voice. "You, however, know the town well. People might be more comfortable talking to you."

I watched him for a moment. Maybe it wasn't wise to trust someone I'd just met with such sensitive information, but I knew deep down I'd need all the help I could get. "All right, Max." I extended my hand across the table. "A free exchange of information henceforth, starting with whatever you know about Neil's mistress."

He shook my hand, holding it just a touch longer than necessary. My cheeks warmed at the contact. "I don't know who Neil was seeing," he explained, "but I do know that he went to the Blue Moon Tavern almost every night. That might be a good place to start. What time do you close up?"

I tilted my head as I returned my hand to my lap. "Why Mr. Howard, are you asking me out for drinks?"

He gave me a half-smile. "Strictly for the investigation, of course."

I stood as a new customer walked in, but kept my eyes on Max. "Pick me up here at seven."

He looked up at me. "What do I owe you for the coffee?"

"It's on the house. I have a feeling you undercharged me for Spooky's shots." I walked away, leaving no room for argument, and met the new customer at the counter.

Not long after I left him, Francis and Elmer invited themselves to Max's table. I *so* did not want to know what they discussed. For a small town, we sure had a lot of matchmakers.

NOT A MINUTE after Max headed out, Detective White came through the door. I had almost forgotten that he intended to come by, and hadn't had time to think about the reason. I resisted the urge to scowl as he approached the counter.

He pursed his full lips while he looked above me at the menu. His eyes drifted down to my face. "What do you recommend?"

I crossed my arms, turning my hips sideways to lean against the counter bordering the wall. "Everything is good. Take your pick."

I didn't quite care for the way he looked at me. It was like he knew exactly what I was thinking. "I feel we might have gotten off on the wrong foot, Ms. O'Shea."

I snorted. "That tends to happen when you accuse people of murder for no good reason. And it's Addy."

His smile was perhaps as charming as Max's. I would have liked it if I didn't think he was just humoring me. "I'm just trying to do my job, Addy. I'm starting to suspect that you're trying to do my job too."

I gave him innocent eyes. "I'm not sure what you mean, detective."

"Well first I see you at Mrs. Howard's house, though she had just finished telling me that she hardly knows you. And then I see Max Howard, the victim's cousin, exiting your cafe."

I wrinkled my nose. "It's a small town, detective. It's not a crime to pay my condolences, nor to serve paying customers."

His eyes had drifted back up to the menu. "I think I'll just take a black coffee."

I pushed away from the counter and put my hands on my hips. "Has anyone ever told you that you're a bit irritating?"

His grin softened his strong features. "I hear it all the time." He leaned his hands on the counter. "I'll level with you, Addy. While I haven't ruled you out, I don't think you're my suspect. I just wanted to come by here to make sure you stay off my case. There's a murderer out there, and getting involved could be dangerous."

More than you know, I thought to myself. I turned to

fix his coffee. "I told you I'm not getting involved, but just out of curiosity, why did you decide to rule me out?" I popped a lid on his coffee, hoping he would take the hint to not linger.

He took the offered cup. "You've lived in Twilight Hollow your entire life. According to anyone I've asked, you don't have a mean bone in your body, though some folk don't care for your brand of sarcasm." He watched me for a moment. "Some people had a few odd things to say, but I haven't heard anything that would imply you might have had a reason to commit murder."

"Odd things?" I asked.

He pulled out his wallet and offered me a five. "Yeah, a few odd things. Some people in town seem to think you and your sisters are witches."

I smirked as I took the offered bill. "And what do *you* think?"

"Yet to be determined. Keep the change." He saluted me with his coffee cup, then turned and walked away, letting himself out the door.

I stared after him, not entirely sure what had just happened. He claimed I wasn't really a suspect, but I got the impression he was still suspicious of me, just maybe not for murder.

A day ago, I would've taken the hint and butted out of the murder investigation now that my name was mostly clear, but not now. Something had chased me home, and I believed that something had everything to do with Neil's murder. It was too big of a coincidence for it to happen just a day after I found Neil.

I might not have had many mean bones in my body, but I also never backed down from a fight.

CHAPTER EIGHT

Max picked me up at seven on the dot. After locking up, we walked across the street to where he'd parked his forest green Jeep Cherokee.

"Do you mind if we swing by my house to check on Spooky?" I asked.

He had already told me yes by the time I realized I had just invited someone who was nearly a stranger to my house. I almost took it back, but I *did* want to check on the cat. Now that I had finally found a familiar, I wasn't about to neglect him.

Plus Francis and Elmer knew I was going to the tavern with Max. If I disappeared, they knew who to point the finger at.

I buckled my seatbelt, then gave him directions to my

house. He had an easy air about him, and no bad vibes whatsoever. I was pretty sure I'd be fine.

The drive only took a couple minutes, and when we pulled up it was clear he intended to wait in his vehicle. That gesture alone banished any remaining paranoia.

I opened the door and got out. "You can come in. I promise not to murder you."

With a smile, he shut off the engine and opened his door, meeting me on the other side of the jeep.

Even though I had felt fine just moments before, I started to feel uneasy as we walked up the driveway, and I didn't think it was because of Max. I was having that dark prickly feeling again. I was only slightly surprised when we reached my front door to find it ajar. The inside of my house was pitch black.

My heart pattered in my throat. "Someone has been here," I whispered.

Max put a hand on my shoulder as I reached for the door. "We should call the police."

"I need to make sure Spooky is okay."

I reached for the door again, but Max beat me to it. "At least let me go in first."

I was able to give him that much, mostly because I was already shaking in my boots. I stepped back as he pushed the door open wide and we both peered into the dark living room. Nothing moved.

Max stepped inside, glancing around cautiously. He flipped on the light switch.

"Meow!" Spooky came running toward us. He ignored Max and ran right out the door, stopping to twine around my feet frantically.

I picked him up, holding him close as Max went further into the house. He went left and flipped on the light in the kitchen, then went the other way to check up the stairs.

I stepped inside with Spooky and shut the door behind me.

A moment later, Max came down the stairs. "The house is empty. It doesn't seem like anything was damaged, though you'll have to be the judge if anything was stolen."

It wasn't a burglar who had broken in, but I didn't know how to tell him that dark magical energy was creeping up and down my arms. Whatever had chased me the previous night had now broken into my home.

After a final glance around, Max came to stand before me and Spooky. "We should call the police."

I gave him a tight smile, mostly to keep my lips from trembling. "No, I must have not shut the door all the way. It doesn't look like anything was messed with, so it was probably just the wind."

I could feel Spooky's little heart pattering against my

hands. It was most certainly not just the wind, but cops wouldn't do me any good here.

"Addy—" he began, ready to argue.

I forced a more genuine smile. "Really, it's fine. I'm terrible at shutting the door all the way. It's old and it tends to catch. But do you mind if we reschedule?"

He stepped forward. "Of course not. Do you want to call someone to stay with you?"

"I'll call my sisters. They live together just a few blocks away." I thought about it. I didn't like involving a non-magical human in this business, but if Spooky was this, well, spooked, I didn't much fancy the thought of being alone. "Do you mind waiting with me until they get here? Then maybe we can do the tavern tomorrow?"

"Of course, and only if you still want to go."

"Of course I still want to go." I turned toward the door and locked it, then turned back to him. "Let's go back into the kitchen and I'll fix us something to eat"

He followed me as I walked past him. In truth, I was now a little worried about going to the tavern tomorrow because I'd have to leave Spooky again, but maybe I could get one of my sisters to watch him. I couldn't let this one little thing scare me off. All of this weirdness had started after I found Neil's body. And if Neil's murderer was the one stalking me, I couldn't waste any time in figuring out just who that was.

THIRTY MINUTES LATER, Luna and Callie were bursting through my door as soon as I unlocked it. Max stepped out of the kitchen, and they both froze.

"Why Addy," Callie said, "I didn't realize you already had company."

Luna, the more polite of the two, walked past me and introduced herself to Max.

I narrowed my eyes at Callie, warning her to be on her best behavior.

Max introduced himself to her too, then stepped toward me. "So I'll see you tomorrow then?"

"It's a date. Thanks for waiting with me." Now that my initial fright had passed, I was feeling silly for having him stay. But at least we'd had a nice dinner together.

I showed him to the door, shutting and locking it after he left, then turned toward my sisters, bracing myself for the onslaught.

Callie crossed her arms and leaned her butt against the arm of my white couch. She lifted a brow. "Awful late to have company. What does he mean about tomorrow?"

Luna had narrowed her eyes. "He introduced himself as Max Howard. Is he any relation to Neil?"

I chewed the inside of my cheek. "Let's make some tea and I'll answer all your questions."

Callie shook her head, tossing her strawberry blonde curls. "I don't think so, Addy. You're not placating us with your tea."

I walked past both of them and flopped on the couch, then clutched a pillow to my chest. Spooky, who'd had enough time to calm down, strutted in from the kitchen and hopped up beside me. I told my sisters everything, starting with the pawnshop being closed and ending with why Max was waiting with me and why I had called them both over. I assumed Callie had already filled Luna in about Sasha.

I ended up with both my sisters staring down at me.

"You think the dark magic following you has something to do with Neil's death?" Luna asked.

I shrugged my shoulders against the couch cushion. "It did all start right after that. Of course, it also started right after I found Spooky." I glanced at the cat curled up beside me.

"I guess it doesn't matter how it started," Callie said, "as long as we're prepared to finish it. We'll ward your house tonight, and one of us will be here at all times in case whatever this is comes back."

Luna sat down beside me, then placed a hand on my leg. "We should probably tell mom."

I gritted my teeth. "We are *not* telling mom. She'll try to make me move back in with her."

"She just worries about you," Luna soothed.

I sunk further down into the couch cushions, glowering. "She worries I can't protect myself since I'm not a proper witch, and me calling you here tonight proves that she's right."

Luna patted my leg. "There are many dark things that mean harm to good witches. You were smart to ask for our help."

"But back to the cute veterinarian," Callie interrupted.

I rolled my eyes and stood. "Now I really do need that tea. Or something stronger."

My sisters followed me into the kitchen. As grumpy as I was at the talk of mom, I was grateful they were both there, and that they would ward my house. A ward should keep out any dark magic, but I wasn't leaving Spooky alone again until the murder was solved and whatever dark thing had broken into my house was banished.

I started making the tea while my sisters went from door to door and window to window, whispering old words and sprinkling herbs. One by one, they warded every entryway.

Spooky stayed near my feet wherever I walked. Something must have scared him badly. I wish he could tell me what it was.

Of course, it couldn't be that easy. Most cats couldn't talk, and dead men like Neil told no tales.

Whatever this dark thing was, it was on a witch hunt, and I was done running.

CHAPTER NINE

I called the vet's office and left a message for Max after draining my first cup of morning coffee. I had forgotten to tell him that Tuesdays were my day off from the cafe. Evie would open in the morning for her shift, then would lock up at noon, so if he tried to go by to pick me up, no one would be there.

Though the wards should protect my house, my sisters and I worked out a schedule where one of us would always be home. I took the first shift today since Callie needed to meet with a client, and Luna had her usual office hours at her therapy practice.

I decided to use my time alone to try out some more baking. That way if it turned out bad, no one would be around to see me fail.

Well, except for Spooky. He sat on the tiled kitchen floor, watching me studiously as I measured out flour for muffins. The only blueberries I had were frozen, but if the recipe worked out, I would buy some fresh berries and bake some muffins to sell at the cafe.

My cell phone rang in my back pocket just as I was pouring the batter into the liners I'd placed in the pan. I wiped my hands on my red and white checkered apron, then answered the phone.

Max's voice came through the other end. "I got your message, it's no problem picking you up at your house. I do, however, have an idea."

I leaned my back against the counter. "Go on."

"My last appointment is at noon, so seeing as we both have the afternoon off, I thought we could do some extra sleuthing. Say 1 o'clock?"

Callie was coming back over at twelve, so that worked out. "What does this extra sleuthing entail?"

"Neil's brother, Desmond, lives over in Wickenburg. I've been meaning to go by and pay my respects, but it would be nice to have a buffer along."

"I take it he's a handful?" I asked.

"Something like that."

I stroked my chin, though he couldn't see it. "So I get to innocently question Neil's brother, and you don't have to go visit him alone."

"Mutually beneficial, don't you think?"

The oven beeped, and I took a moment to slide the

pan of muffin batter in. "He doesn't happen to like blueberry muffins, does he?"

"I have no idea. Why?"

I shut the oven door, then knelt down to pet Spooky, hoping his presence would make the muffins as good as the cookies had been. "People tend to talk more when there are baked goods and coffee around."

"I'd wager Desmond would prefer whiskey, but muffins probably wouldn't hurt."

"It's a date then. I'll see you at one, and we can go to the tavern afterward."

I could almost hear him smiling. "Two dates in one day, how lucky."

We said our goodbyes and hung up, then I lifted Spooky into my arms. "We are going to make some progress today," I said. "I feel it."

Danger, a voice whispered in my mind.

My eyes wide, I looked down at the cat. "Did you say something?"

His amber eyes stared back at me.

I shrugged. "Must have just been my imagination. Let's go pick out something to wear for my dates."

I let Spooky down to the floor and gave him a stroke, wondering if it really had been my imagination, or if my familiar was trying to warn me of something.

There was little I could do about it now. The house

was warded, and Callie would be here to watch over Spooky while I was out with Max.

Surely nothing bad could happen in broad daylight with other people around, could it?

Of course, I'd been wrong more than a few times before.

MAX PULLED up at 1 o'clock on the dot. Punctuality wasn't my strong suit, but I could appreciate it in others. It was nice that he made the effort.

I had dressed in a form-fitting taupe sweater that went well with my ginger hair and made my hazel eyes look more green. Fresh black jeans and low-heeled black boots completed the look. If Max could make an effort, so could I. Callie had beamed with fashionista pride when she arrived earlier.

I pushed my loose curls behind my ears as I went to answer the door.

Max stood outside wearing a fisherman's sweater so dark green it was almost black, paired with jeans. He raked fingers through his hair. "Something smells good."

I stepped aside. "That would be the muffins I mentioned. Come on in."

His shoes tapped across my hardwood floor as Spooky came into the room to join us.

"I'll just pack up the muffins and grab my coat," I said, heading into the kitchen. It wasn't cool enough for the coat now, but if we were out late, I would need it.

I moved a little faster to package up the muffins as I heard Callie coming down the stairs. The last thing I needed was her making any implications to Max.

I grabbed my cropped wool coat and purse from where I left them hanging by the door, flinging both over my arm, then balanced two to-go cups of coffee on my packaged up muffins and headed into the living room.

Max was sitting on the couch, with Callie facing him on one of the matching cushioned chairs with her boots up on my coffee table.

"Shoes down," I said, moving to stand in front of the table. I set the muffins and coffee down, then handed Max one cup. "I wasn't sure how you took it, but you liked the latte, so I figured cream was okay."

Max stood to take the cup. "Cream is perfect, I appreciate it."

Callie watched us with a contented smile. "You kids have fun now."

I shot her a quick glare. "I would say the same to you, but I don't want my house to get destroyed." I gave Max a much more pleasant expression. "Ready?"

"As I'll ever be." He said goodbye to Callie, then took his coffee toward the door, holding it open for me since my hands were full with the muffins and my cup.

His jeep was parked on the street out front, since my and Callie's cars took up the driveway. He held the Jeep door open for me as we reached it. I really wasn't a fan of all the door holding, but my hands *were* full, so I couldn't exactly argue.

"Still shaken up about last night?" he asked once we were buckled in and driving down the street.

My brows shot up just as I was about to take a sip of coffee. "What makes you say that?"

"You have your sister staying home while you're away."

"How about you be a little less observant?" I smiled and sipped my coffee. "I'm sure there's nothing to be concerned about, but with her there, at least I won't worry." I laughed. "Well I won't worry about anyone breaking in. There are plenty of *other* things to worry about with Callie around."

He grinned as he took a left that would eventually lead us to the two lane highway. "Yeah, I got that impression. It's nice that you guys are close though. I'd love to have close family like that."

"No siblings?"

He shook his head, keeping his eyes on the road. "Just my cousins, and they're the type I would only see on holidays growing up. And now I have one less of them."

"But you didn't grow up here," I said.

"Nope, born and raised in Sacramento, but my dad grew up here. He and Ike had inherited the family home, and they left it to me when my dad passed."

I slowly pieced together the puzzle of the Howard family in my head. "Were Desmond and Neil upset that you got the house?"

He shrugged. "I'm sure they were, but I didn't hear anything about it. They probably didn't want to cause trouble and have Ike cut them out entirely."

I sipped my coffee as I thought things over. "So both Desmond and Neil depended on their dad for extra money."

He glanced at me as we pulled up to a stop sign. "Are you interrogating me, Ms. O'Shea?"

I laughed. "Sorry, it's just an interesting situation. Sasha told me Ike bailed her out financially when she and Neil split up. She made it seem like he had finally decided to cut Neil off."

"Now that's news to me. Ike has always been around to bail out his sons. He did like Sasha though. He'd hoped she'd be a good influence on Neil."

I pursed my lips, wondering if Sasha could have been the motivation for murder. Would someone have wanted to protect her enough to get rid of Neil? Of course, she had already kicked him out, and her finances were separate from his. She didn't exactly need any more saving.

As we took the highway east toward Wickenburg, I

had another thought. "So Desmond lives in Wickenburg. Isn't that where Sasha has her jewelry boutique?"

He glanced at me as we changed lanes. "You really are interrogating me. You might want to be a little more subtle with Desmond. He tends to be suspicious."

I fought my blush. "Sorry, I'm a little single focused. It's a bad habit of mine."

"Oh no, don't get me wrong, that's what I like about you. I just figured I better warn you about Desmond. And yes, Sasha's boutique is in Wickenburg."

I relaxed a little, glad I had agreed to sharing the investigation with Max. Much better than sharing it with Logan White, not that he'd let me in on things to begin with.

I settled more comfortably into my seat with the muffins balanced on my leg. "Anyhow," I drew out the word, "you inherited the family home, and that's what made you decide to start your practice in Twilight Hollow?"

He took the exit to Wickenburg. "That was part of it. I was also tired of the city, and my dad always reminisced about Twilight Hollow. When he passed, it seemed like a good time to make a change."

I wasn't sure what to say. I never knew what to say in these situations. I'd never been a big sharer, so it always surprised me when other people were more forthcoming. "I'm sorry for your loss." The words seemed trite. I barely remembered my dad, and I wasn't sure what I would do when my mom passed away. Just thinking about it made me feel guilty for not visiting her more.

"Thanks," he said, not seeming offended by my lack of meaningful response. We pulled up to a trailer court, driving slow between the mobile homes before stopping in a narrow gravel drive.

He put the Jeep in park and turned off the engine. "I told Desmond I was bringing someone, but he doesn't know it's the person who found Neil's body. You might want to keep that to yourself."

I made a gesture of zipping my lips, locking them, and tossing away the key, then opened my door before Max could come around and do it for me.

We left what remained of our coffees in the car and walked together up the drive with me carrying the muffins.

The door opened before we reached it. I had never met Desmond Howard before, but I could see the family resemblance, at least between him and Neil. He was a slightly taller, slightly thinner version of the dead man, with a halo of dark, thin hair around his balding scalp.

He put on a smile, but I hadn't missed the brief glare he gave Max. He was either jealous of his cousin, or still upset about the family home. Probably both.

He came down the stairs and offered me his hand. "Desmond Howard, nice to meet you."

I hesitated. Max said not to let him know I was the one who found the body, but Sasha and Neil had both been told my name. Logan would be a pretty shoddy detective if he hadn't questioned Desmond too.

I shook his hand. "Callie, pleased to meet you."

Max cast a glance my way, then put on a quick smile. "I was sorry to hear about Neil. How are you holding up?"

Desmond waved him off. "I hadn't even spoken to him in months. I'd say his death was no great loss to the world. Why don't you two come in?"

I kept my smile in place as we walked up the thin wooden stairs into his home, though I desperately wanted to know what Max thought of Desmond's blatant dismissal of his own brother's death. I flinched as the door shut behind us, then I took a quick look around, trying to memorize all the details.

The inside of his home was surprisingly clean. I don't know why I had expected otherwise, maybe because Desmond himself didn't appear terribly clean with his yellowed white tee shirt and grease-stained jeans. It was a strange juxtaposition. I thought of Sasha's clean house, and her jewelry boutique not being far off, then pushed the thought away. I wasn't desperate enough to jump to such wild conclusions, not just yet.

Desmond offered us seats at his little kitchenette.

I placed the muffins on the table. "I'm not sure if you like blueberries, but I figured I'd give it a shot."

Desmond gave me a suspicious look, like bringing him baked goods was something out of the ordinary.

My gut clenched. Had my first thought been right? Had Sasha been here? Had she told him that Adelaide O'Shea had brought her cookies and asked too many questions about Neil's murder?

He sat and took one of the offered muffins, and the moment passed. As soon as he took a bite, the suspicious glint went out of his eyes.

I took the seat across from Desmond, leaving Max to sit between us. The two started reminiscing about holidays spent together growing up. It almost sounded like they had once been friends, but bitterness and jealousy had tainted the relationship.

Unfortunately, he didn't tell us much we didn't already know, and he was adamant that he and Neil hadn't spoken in months. He never mentioned Sasha.

"So have you been out to see my old man yet?" he asked once the tray of muffins had been demolished to nothing but crumbs.

"Not yet," Max said. "I'll probably head out that way in the morning."

Desmond shivered. "Good luck with that, those woods give me the creeps."

"What woods?" I blurted.

Both men looked at me like I had just appeared.

"The woods just west of Twilight Hollow," Desmond answered. "There are a few houses out there. That's where my dad lives."

I bit my tongue before I could say anything. I knew the woods well. My mom had grown up out there, and had moved back to the family home when she retired. I felt the same way about the area as Desmond. It was part of why I didn't visit my mom nearly as much as I should, though I had never mentioned the strange feeling to anyone.

I retreated within my thoughts while the men continued the conversation. At this point, I was pretty sure we had nothing else to learn from Desmond, at least not about the murder. Though it was interesting Ike would choose to live in the woods when he could've kept the family home instead of giving it to Max.

Eventually we said our goodbyes, and we thanked Desmond for having us. Any suspicion he had initially felt seemed to be gone, and I wondered how much of that was a result of my muffins, and how much of it was just being around family. Despite their differences, Max and Desmond still shared a bond. It made me hope Desmond wasn't the murderer. Max had already lost one cousin, he didn't need to lose them both.

CHAPTER TEN

Despite the hours of reminiscence, Desmond seemed relieved to shut the door behind us. We walked down the gravel drive just as an unmarked police car pulled up.

"You've got to be kidding me," I groaned.

Max stopped beside me. "Friend of yours?"

"Hardly," I grumbled as Logan stepped out of his car.

"Ms. O'Shea," he said as he approached us. "Why am I not surprised?"

I plastered a smile on my face. "We were just leaving."

"Not so fast." He looked to Max. "Do you mind giving us a moment alone?"

I nodded to Max that it was all right, though I wanted nothing more than to hop in his Jeep and flee the scene.

Max climbed into the driver's seat and shut the door, leaving me alone with the detective and my empty muffin tray.

Logan glanced at Desmond's home. "Let's take a walk."

I allowed him to guide me down the narrow street bisecting rows of mobile homes.

When we were out of sight and earshot of Desmond's windows, Logan stopped walking and turned to me. "What are you doing here, Addy?"

I forced myself to meet his chocolate brown eyes, and decided on a half-truth. "Max didn't want to come alone, so I came for moral support. What are *you* doing here?"

"I had a few extra questions for Mr. Howard, not that it's any of your concern."

"Is he a suspect?"

Logan's eyes narrowed. "For someone staying out of my case, you sure are showing a lot of interest in it."

I batted my lashes. "Can't blame a girl for being curious, can you?"

"I most certainly can, but since you're already here, did you learn anything from Mr. Howard?"

My jaw went slack. "I thought you didn't want me involved."

He stepped a little closer, shielding my expression from Max's view a few driveways behind us. "No, I don't want you involved, but seeing as you're here anyways, I may as well hear what you've learned."

I shut my jaw with a click. I didn't want to tell him anything, just out of spite, but at the end of the day I wanted the murder solved. Now was not the time to be petty. "He claims he hasn't seen his brother in months, that they had a falling out. He didn't seem to know who would want to kill Neil. Though oddly, he avoided talk of Sasha."

His brows lifted. "That's new information. Why do you think that is?"

I wasn't sure if he was just humoring me, and I felt silly for even considering voicing my earlier thoughts. But what if I was right? It could help the investigation to at least look into it. "I was surprised at the cleanliness of Desmond's home. It's not just normal clean, it's nitpicky clean. I remembered Sasha's house was the same way, and she does run a business out here."

He watched me for a moment, giving me no clues as to what he was thinking. "Thanks for your time." He gestured for me to start walking back toward Max's Jeep.

With my muffin tray in one hand, I crossed my arms and jutted out my hip. "What gives? I just gave you good information."

"That's what you're supposed to do when the police question you."

I scowled. "You're insufferable." I gave in and started

walking, but stopped as another thought crossed my mind.

Logan looked at me in question.

I chewed my lip. He probably wasn't going to like this. "Can you at least do me one small favor? You know, for all that information?"

He sighed. "That depends on the favor."

"If you mention me to Desmond, he thinks my name is Callie."

Even though I was embarrassed, I took a measure of satisfaction that his thoughts were actually readable for once, as his eyes flew wide and his jaw dropped. "If you were just coming to give your condolences, why did you lie about your name?"

I crossed my arms. "Well it seems like you've been giving my name to everyone you question, so I assumed Desmond would know it too and might not want to invite me in."

His brow creased. "Addy, I haven't been giving anyone your name. Twilight Hollow is a small town, everyone already knew you found the body."

I frowned. I had been perfectly happy blaming Logan.

He watched me for a moment longer. "Fine, as far as I'm concerned, your name is Callie."

I grinned. "I take back what I said, you're only *mostly* insufferable."

FAMILIAR SPIRITS

We started walking again. I heard an engine rev, then I heard the tires screech behind me.

I didn't have time to react. Logan grabbed my arm and flung us both toward the side of the road. We landed hard in the grass as a white truck went screeching by.

My breath heaved. Lying on my side, I met Logan's eyes for a second, then he was up on his feet, peering after the truck with one hand up shielding the sun.

I rolled over to find Max running toward me. He knelt by my side. "Addy, Addy. Are you alright?"

I blinked up at him. "Did that truck just try to hit me?"

Logan's shadow loomed over us. "It tried to hit us both." I sat up as he looked to Max. "Did you catch the license plate?"

Max shook his head. "I only looked up when I heard the tires screeching, then I ran straight over here to make sure Addy was okay. I didn't even see the vehicle."

Logan sucked his teeth. If he was at all shaken up about almost dying, he didn't show it. "Get her out of here," he said to Max. "Take her somewhere safe. I'll be in touch soon."

He was walking away with a cell phone to his ear before either of us could reply.

Max put a hand on my back. "Can you stand?"

I nodded, trying to determine if I was hurt, but I just felt numb and shaky.

He helped me up, then walked with me back to the Jeep. This time I was more than happy to let him open my door for me. I had lost my muffin tray somewhere in the grass, but decided it wasn't that important.

Once we were out on the road driving away from the trailer court, I finally started to relax.

I could not say the same for Max. Tension radiated from his clenched jaw and stiff shoulders as he took a few turns until we were back out on the highway. "Where do you want to go? I'll stay with you until the detective calls."

I stared at him. "We're going to the tavern, remember?"

"Addy, I don't think that's such a good idea."

I jutted my chin out. "Max, I need a drink, and it's no crime for the two of us to go to the tavern. It's safer to wait in a public place anyway."

He glanced at with me with both his hands grasped around the wheel. "I guess you're right, but just for a drink. No questioning anyone about Neil."

"Why?"

"Addy, someone just tried to run you over. What if the murderer knows you're trying to find them?"

I winced. He had a point. Maybe I was being too obvious about things. Asking questions at the tavern would only make me a bigger target. "I guess you're right."

"So no questions?"

I sunk down further in my seat. "Throw in a meal and we have an agreement."

He glanced at me again, this time with a small smile. "You could eat after nearly dying?"

"You guys ate all the muffins."

He laughed. "You're one of a kind, Adelaide O'Shea. Drinks and a meal it is."

We spent the rest of the drive in companionable silence, which was for the best, because my thoughts were a mess. I hadn't sensed any dark magic when that person tried to run us over, which meant the driver had been a mundane. Could more than one person or thing be gunning for me?

I guessed it didn't really matter. It was too late to turn back now.

CHAPTER ELEVEN

As soon as we arrived at the tavern, I went to the bathroom to call Callie. After ensuring that all was well at my home, I told her what happened.

"What!" I pulled the phone away from my ear at her shrieking, then brought it back when it seemed she was done. "Why didn't you start with that?"

"I'm okay, I'm at the tavern with Max, but I wanted to warn you. If someone is after me, they might come to my house. Maybe you should take Spooky somewhere else."

"No way, let them come," she growled. "I'll be here waiting for them."

"At least call Luna over," I sighed.

"She's already on her way. We were going to have a movie night."

The tension in my jaw relaxed. They were both formidable witches. Together they should be fine, especially with Luna there. "Alright, be safe. We're going to wait here until Logan calls us."

"And he was the one who pushed you out of the way?" she asked before I could hang up.

"The truck was aiming for both of us, so he got us both out of the way."

She let out a low whistle. "Addy, he saved your life. You're going to have to be nicer to him."

Dang it, she was right. "I'll talk to you soon."

"When you're done at the tavern, have Max bring you straight home. Your cat misses you."

I smirked. "Bye Callie."

"Bye sis."

I hung up and tossed my cell phone into my purse, then took a look in the mirror. My jeans were dark enough to not show the grass stains, but my sweater didn't fare quite as well. I leaned forward, tugging a dried leaf from my hair.

When I was as presentable as I was going to get, I went out into the tavern.

The tavern was a long rectangle, the bar on one side and tables on the other. At the back were pool tables and dart boards. Though it was only 5 o'clock, the dark glass and dimmed lighting put the tavern in perpetual twilight. People were already getting loud, some voices slurred. Max sat reading a menu at a table near the bar.

I approached and sat down, taking up the other menu. When the server came, I ordered a burger and an IPA. Max ordered fish and chips and the same beer as me.

We handed off our menus, and I was about to speak when I noticed a woman staring at us from the bar. I'd seen her around town a few times, and I thought her name was Mary.

Max followed my gaze. "Why is that woman staring at me?"

I realized that she was, in fact, staring at Max. It only looked like she was staring at us both because she had to look past me to see him. "I have no idea, but I think we're about to find out."

She had slid down from her bar stool to march toward us. She was small, probably only 5'2" with boots that made her look taller. The crimson blouse she wore was perfect for her dark eyes and hair, and her pale skin. She seemed in her late thirties, though with her thick makeup it was hard to tell.

She stopped in front of our table with her hands on her hips and looked down at Max. "You Neil's cousin?"

He frowned. "Yes?"

Her eyes narrowed. "Neil owed me five weeks

backpay when someone bumped him off. I'd say it's his family's responsibility to make good on his debts."

I cleared my throat to get her attention. "You worked for Neil?"

When those dark eyes landed on me I regretted speaking. "Yeah, I answered phones and did the billing at the auto shop. What's it to you?"

"Can you think of anyone who would have wanted to hurt him?"

"Addy," Max warned.

She looked back and forth between the two of us. "Sure, I can think of people who would want to hurt him. Me, for one, seeing as he owed me. His ex-wife, he was always running around on her. And his brother Desmond. He came into the shop real angry the day before Neil died."

Max and I locked gazes. Hadn't Desmond just told us he hadn't seen his brother in months?

"What about my money?" she pressed. "Tammy says I can work tables here, but it'll take a while for me to save up enough for rent. I support my daughter on my own, and I'd rather she not be homeless."

"How much does he owe you?" I asked.

"Ten bucks an hour, twenty hours a week, for five weeks."

I wrinkled my nose. Leave it to Neil to pay her under minimum wage when she had a daughter to support. He was probably paying her under the table too.

Max handed her a business card. "I'm visiting Neil's dad tomorrow. I'm sure he and I can figure something out for you."

She took the card, seeming a little stunned he had actually agreed to help her. "Well . . . thanks then. I'm Mary by the way." She looked the card over again. "I'll call you tomorrow."

"Hey Mary?" I asked before she could walk back to the bar.

She pursed her lips. "Yes?"

"Do you have any idea why Desmond was so upset with Neil?"

She shook her head. "No idea, though I know Neil was real upset with him too."

"Do you know the names of any other women he was seeing beside Sasha?"

She shrugged. "I figured that was none of my business. He hit on me a time or two, but my ex set him straight."

I lifted a brow. "Your ex?"

"My boyfriend then, my ex now. Blake Monroe." She looked to Max. "I'll call you tomorrow."

I watched her as she walked back to the bar, but I could feel Max staring at me. "What happened to not asking questions about Neil?"

I turned and gave him innocent eyes. "But it was such a good opportunity. Look at all we learned."

The server came back with our drinks, placed a frosted glass in front of each of us, then retreated.

Max rubbed a hand across his face and shook his head. "What am I going to do with you?"

I drained half my beer in three gulps, then set down my glass. "Well first, I think you're going to buy me another drink."

The alcohol washed away the rest of my jitters, replacing them with excitement. Desmond had lied about seeing his brother, and Mary had just confirmed that Blake Monroe was a meaningful suspect.

Max sighed. "At least promise you'll take me with you when you question Desmond and Blake Monroe."

I grinned. "As long as you take me with you tomorrow to see Ike."

He shook his head and smiled as the server delivered our food. The burger smelled heavenly after a long day of only muffins for sustenance. As soon as the server was gone, I lifted it and took a bite. *Divine.*

Max watched me. "You're making that look like the best burger you've ever eaten."

I swallowed the bite then set the burger down. "Do you ever stop and think about just how amazing food is? How we can make so many different flavors, and how those flavors can actually inspire emotions?"

He looked down at his fish and chips. "You know, I've never actually thought of it that way."

"It's the whole reason I opened my cafe. I love that cozy feeling that tea and coffee can provide, and I wanted to do that for other people too. You don't have to be a brain surgeon or a politician to make a difference in the world."

He ate a fry, chewing slow and thoughtful, then shrugged. "I've got nothing. Not half as good as your muffins."

Smiling, I took another sip of my half-empty beer, then turned at the sound of the door opening. In walked Logan White, and he did *not* look happy.

He quickly spotted us and approached our table. "You're not answering your phone."

My brows knit together. I placed my purse on my lap then dug around until I found my phone. Sure enough, three missed calls. "Sorry, I couldn't hear it over the noise." I waved one hand toward the bar, which was slowly filling up. "How did you find us?"

Logan remained standing, though there was a free chair. "I went by your house. Your sister told me where you were. She also mentioned that someone broke into your house the other night."

My mouth twisted. Curse Callie and her big mouth. "I don't know that someone broke in. I probably just didn't shut the door all the way. Nothing was missing."

Finally, he pulled out the third chair and sat. He leaned forward across the open space on the table and lowered his voice, "Addy, someone tried to kill you today. You need to take these things more seriously."

I would have told him that I was taking it seriously, and that I had made my sisters ward every door and window in my house, but I was pretty sure he already thought I was a nut. I didn't need to further those suspicions.

I lifted my hands in surrender. "Alright, you win. I'll be careful."

"I'll be placing an officer to watch your house tonight, just in case."

I batted my eyelashes. "If that will make you feel better, detective, I'll take it."

"And I'll be driving you home as soon as you finish your meal."

Now that made me frown. "I'm sure Max won't mind dropping me off."

Logan lowered his chin. "Have you considered the fact that being around you is dangerous to him?"

"Now wait—" Max began.

I rubbed my brow, then shook my head at Max, realizing I'd been foolish. "He's totally right. I'm sorry, I hadn't thought of it that way."

"Addy, it's fine, I can take care of myself."

I looked down at my burger. Suddenly it didn't seem

so appetizing. "No, no one can protect themselves from the type of person who would hit a detective and a civilian with a truck just to get them out of the way."

Max opened his mouth, but no further argument came out.

I felt awful. I was okay with risking my life, but not with risking Max's. I turned to Logan. "You can drive me home."

"She sees reason, what a surprise."

I glared. "Don't push it." I waved the server over, then asked for a box for my food. I turned to Max. "I've got cash for my half."

He shook his head. "Don't worry about it, it's on me."

Logan watched the exchange silently. Once the server had returned and my food was boxed up, Logan and I stood.

"Call me tomorrow?" I said hopefully to Max.

"Of course."

We said our goodbyes and left. I had a feeling I would no longer be joining Max to visit Ike. Even if he was still okay with it, what if me being around him really did risk his life? I was already in this thing, but Max didn't have to be.

Of course, visiting Ike on my own wasn't out of the question. If he lived out near my mom, I could just happen by on the way to visit her.

Though that meant I should probably actually visit

her, and that meant traveling through the creepy woods there and back. Even worse, my mom would know something was up, and she would make me tell her. Once I told her, she'd try to convince me to stay with her, but that was an issue where I would put my foot down. My mom had only ever tried to protect me, to shield me since my magic was so weak, but I had a familiar now. I was a real witch, and I could take care of myself.

CHAPTER TWELVE

I sat in Logan's unmarked car with my boxed up burger in my lap. His attention was on the road, though we were only going about twenty miles per hour. I could have cut the tension with a knife. The sun was beginning to set, casting the neighborhood in shades of pink and orange.

I jumped when Logan finally spoke. "I'm assuming it's no coincidence you ended up at the same tavern Neil frequented."

I gnawed my lower lip. "There aren't many places to get a good burger in town."

He laughed and shook his head, relaxing his shoulders a bit. "You may as well tell me what you learned."

I lifted a brow. "Oh really? You want my help?"

"Another perspective on the case is welcome, especially when you've already paid the price of endangering yourself."

I rolled my eyes. "The woman who worked for Neil recognized Max tonight. She claimed Neil owed her five weeks of pay. She also claimed that Neil hit on her before, and that her boyfriend at the time, Blake Monroe, set him straight. Which is odd, considering Sasha told me Blake had been involved in one of Neil's money-making schemes. Then there's Desmond. He told us he hadn't seen Neil in months, but Mary said Desmond had come to the shop to argue with Neil shortly before his death."

"Does this Mary have a last name?"

I stared at him for a moment, trying to judge his expression, then smiled. "Could it be I have discovered information you didn't already know?"

"Legally Neil had no employees. He must have been paying Mary under the table, so no, I didn't know she existed."

"He was also paying her below minimum wage. She's supposed to call Max tomorrow, I'm sure he could get her information for you."

We pulled up to my house. Logan shut off the engine. "I'll wait out here until the officer arrives."

I stared at him. "You know, you're not very good at saying thank you."

His smile was a brief flicker in the growing darkness. "Neither are you, Ms. O'Shea."

I couldn't help but laugh. "You may as well come in until the officer arrives. If you don't, Luna will just come back out here and drag you by the collar."

Now it was his turn to stare. "Seriously?"

"Seriously. And haven't you heard? It's bad luck to cross Luna O'Shea. Now let's go." I lifted my boxed up burger from my lap, slung my purse over my shoulder, and opened the door.

The chilly night air clamped around me as we exited the car, and I realized I'd left my coat in Max's Jeep. We walked up the driveway and went through the unlocked front door to find Callie and Luna curled up on the couch with a massive bowl of popcorn between them. Spooky was curled up on the other side of Luna. A romcom played on my small TV.

My sisters looked up, both with green clay face masks and braids in their hair.

"Why hello again, detective," Callie said, not embarrassed in the least.

Luna stretched out her sweatpants-clad legs, crossing her ankles on top of the coffee table. "I see you've found our delinquent sister."

I locked the door behind us, shaking my head. "Let's go into the kitchen."

Grinning from ear to ear, Logan followed me as I led the way. Spooky hopped off the couch as we passed, trotting into the kitchen just ahead of me.

I put a kettle on while Logan walked around a small dining area. He looked down at one kitchen windowsill, running his finger across it to pick up a few flakes of scattered herbs. He observed them thoughtfully.

"Tea or coffee?" I asked, hoping to distract him.

He dusted the herbs off his fingertips, then turned to me with a raised brow. "Isn't it too late for coffee?"

"Only if you're a foolish mortal."

He laughed. "Coffee it is then."

Spooky had hopped up on the table to examine our new guest. Logan reached out a tentative hand, which Spooky sniffed, then rubbed his nose against.

Shaking my head, I turned my attention to the coffee. I ground fresh beans, then measured the grinds into a French press.

I had just poured the hot water when Spooky hissed. I whipped around, worried he was trying to claw Logan, but he was looking out the dark window.

Logan peered with him. "Stay here, Addy. I think I see something outside."

Goosebumps prickled up my skin as an uneasy feeling clenched my gut. I heard my sisters whispering in the other room before hurrying into the kitchen.

"Addy," Callie said, her voice low with warning.

"I know." I walked toward Logan. "You're going to have to trust me, detective, but we need to stay in the house."

Spooky had arched his back and was spitting at the window. The frame started shaking.

Logan drew his gun and stepped back. "Everyone, behind me!"

Spooky hopped down from the table and hurried back to me, almost as if he had understood Logan's words. I picked him up, then looked to my sisters standing on either side of me in their ridiculous face masks.

I felt a surge of dark power, then the window shattered, raining glass into the kitchen. Logan stood with his gun pointed at a white transparent shape floating through the window.

I swallowed a lump in my throat. It was a ghost, but ghosts weren't supposed to be this powerful. Especially the ghost of a mundane man like Neil Howard.

Logan seemed frozen, but he didn't back down. He pointed his gun at the ghost. "Don't take another step."

Neil's white spectral form leered at the detective, then looked past him to me. "Time to pay for my death, little witch."

My eyes flew wide. Why was he looking at me when he said that? He floated past Logan, who followed him with his gun, but there was nothing to shoot at. The ghost was entirely incorporeal.

I put Spooky down and took both my sister's hands.

The moment the cat curled around my leg, magic flowed through me. We began to chant.

Neil stopped moving toward us, raising his hands to push against the invisible barrier we had formed.

Logan stepped back toward the broken window, watching us with wide eyes, his gun forgotten in his hand.

We continued to chant, an old ritual to banish angry spirits.

Neil started shrieking. He pushed against the barrier, his transparent features contorted with rage.

An unearthly wind kicked up, pushing him back. He slowly lost his hold on the mundane world. In my mind, it was like prying his fingers up one by one.

A magical breeze picked up locks of my hair as we continued our chant. The wind gave a sudden gust, carrying what remained of Neil's spectral form back out the window.

The wind died down.

My hands clasped in either of my sisters' trembled. "How did the ghost just do that? How did he get past the wards?"

"That wasn't a normal ghost," Luna said. "Something dark was giving it power."

Callie dropped my hand. "I think we have a more pressing problem, ladies."

Logan was staring at us, his gun lowered, but not put

away. His bronze skin had gone three shades paler. He shook his head as his eyes landed solely on me. "What did I just see?"

I gnawed my lip, trying to think of a plausible reply. "An elaborate prank?"

He shook his head, glancing at the broken window before taking a step toward us. "That thing—That thing looked like the ghost of Neil Howard."

I glanced at each of my sisters. Luna furrowed her brow, and Callie shrugged. I looked back to Logan. "I'm not quite sure what to tell you, detective."

He glanced at the window again, at a loss. "Did I really just see that?"

I turned toward the kitchen counter. "Why don't I make us some tea?"

He turned and took another step toward us. "Why did that thing think you needed to pay for Neil's murder?"

I took a deep, steadying breath. "I don't know."

A knock at the front door interrupted us.

Logan glanced that way, then put his gun up. "We are not done talking about this." He went to answer the door.

As soon as he was gone, I turned toward my sisters. "What was that? What should we do?"

Callie took my hand and squeezed it. "I don't think

we're going to be able to convince him that his eyes were just playing tricks on him."

I didn't think so either, but that meant I would have to tell him the truth, at least in part. He'd probably try to have me committed. I heard him in the other room telling his officer everything was fine, and to wait outside.

The door shut, and I went to meet him in the living room with Spooky following at my heels. Logan and I both looked at each other, and I just wasn't sure what to say.

He glanced at my sisters as they came to stand in the kitchen doorway, then back to me. "Alright, Ms. O'Shea, I think it's time you told me everything, from the beginning."

I crossed my arms to keep my hands from shaking, then took a deep breath. "Alright, detective. You might want to sit down for this."

CHAPTER THIRTEEN

"Are you sure you don't want some tea?" I asked again, curling my legs on my living room chair, teacup in hand.

Logan sat on the couch stiff-backed, hands grasped on knees. "All I want right now is an explanation." He had sent the officer scheduled to watch the house home, saying he would take the first shift himself. Apparently he intended to use that time to interrogate us.

Callie leaned against the wall near the kitchen entryway. She had washed off her face mask, and changed back into jeans and a long-sleeved tee shirt. "Just tell him, Addy. We have more important things to discuss." Her words were punctuated with Luna banging a hammer in the kitchen, putting boards left over from my new back fencing over the broken window.

I set my tea on the coffee table, then leaned back.

"What you saw was indeed a ghost, but it wasn't a normal ghost. Normal ghosts can't shatter windows. Something is making this ghost stronger than it should be."

Spooky hopped in my lap and curled up. I stroked him absentmindedly as I waited for Logan to reply.

He rubbed his face with his hands and shook his head. "This doesn't make any sense. I can believe that ghosts are real, but this sort of thing just doesn't happen. Ghosts are supposed to be something you just see out of the corner of your eye, something that can't hurt you."

I glanced at Callie, who shrugged. Having him already believe in ghosts was at least a good start.

"I think you know what you saw," I said to Logan. "Now you can either listen to my explanation, or you can forget about it and pretend it never happened. None of us will fault you for the latter."

He lifted his head from his hands. "I wish I could forget, but that's not going to happen. Especially not since the ghost accused you of murdering him."

My mouth went dry. I was hoping he would forget that part. "I told you, I don't know why he said that."

Luna came back into the room with her hammer in hand. "I can tell you why he said that. Someone is manipulating that ghost. They are making him believe that you killed him, and they are giving him the power to retaliate." She gave me a meaningful look. "Someone or something wants you gone, Addy. Or they at least want you scared."

The wheels seemed to turn in Logan's mind as he watched us. "If all of that is true, what about the break-in? Why would this . . . *ghost* snoop around your house if it already knew you murdered it?"

It was my turn to bury my face in my hands. "I don't know. Maybe he was looking for proof that I murdered him." I lifted my head to meet Logan's waiting gaze. "But there was nothing to find, because I did *not* murder him."

He watched me for a moment. "So say I believe all of this, what or who made the ghost think you murdered it?"

I glanced to my sisters. "That's what we need to find out."

"How?" Logan asked.

Luna lowered her chin and gave me a knowing look. "It's time to call mom, Addy. We can't go down to that grave without her."

I flopped back against my chair. She was right.

"Has Neil's body even been buried yet?" Callie asked. "That could pose a problem if it hasn't."

Logan watched with wide eyes as our world unfolded before him. "The body was buried yesterday after the medical examiner released it. The widow declined the opportunity to organize a funeral."

"Call mom," I groaned. "I want to seal Neil in his grave before he gets the strength to come back."

Logan stood abruptly. "You're telling me that thing can come back?"

"We banished it temporarily," Luna explained. "We still need to bind it to its grave. If we're lucky, whoever is controlling it will show themselves then." She pulled her cell phone from her pocket and went into the kitchen, presumably to call our mother.

Spooky nudged my hand for more pets.

Logan was looking back-and-forth between me and Callie. "How can you both be so calm? You're talking about going to a graveyard to bind a ghost and draw out someone who wants Addy dead."

I leaned my head back to look up at him. "Glad to see you still care."

He rolled his eyes. "I know you're not the murderer, Addy. I trust my gut, but I still don't understand how you can be so calm about this, how this all seems so normal to you."

Callie laughed as she pushed away from the wall. "Hasn't anyone told you, detective? We're witches." She strolled into the kitchen, leaving me alone with Logan.

He stared at me. "Was she joking?"

I probably should have been worried about revealing our secret to Logan, but I was too tired and shaken up to care. "What do you think?"

He sat back down and went quiet.

I pet Spooky, giving Logan time to process. There wasn't much else for me to say.

For better or for worse, the cat was out of the bag.

FORTY-FIVE MINUTES later the matriarch of our little clan walked through my front door. She was tall and wiry like Callie, but she had my ginger hair, and Luna's chocolate brown eyes. She wore a flowy, patterned dress done in earth tones, with a deep green cardigan on top.

Though I stood back with both my sisters, my mom's attention went straight to me. "You should have called sooner, Addy."

I glowered. "I was handling it just fine until Neil's ghost showed up."

My mother waved me off as Logan stood from the couch.

"You must be the detective." She walked across the room toward him. "Welcome to our world. I'm Imogene O'Shea." She held his offered hand a little bit too long, and I wondered what sort of reading she was getting from Logan.

My mom's gifts weren't as strong as Luna's in that department, but she had been practicing them a lot longer. Any of us could have worked on the psychic side of our gifts if we wanted to, but we all had our own natural inclinations. My mom's was working with the dead.

Logan furrowed his brow as he took back his hand, and I once again wondered if he could sense a hint of magic. He'd had the same expression when he first shook Callie's hand.

As my mom turned away from Logan, Spooky came in from the kitchen, rubbing his body against the wall of the entryway.

She crouched down in front of him. "Ah, the new familiar. It's nice to see you again."

I stared at her back. "What do you mean *again*?"

She stroked Spooky's fur, then stood to face me. "This cat was once my sister's familiar. She had him when we were kids."

I was so stunned, all I could do was just stand there like an idiot blinking at her. My mom's sister had died when they were teenagers, so I'd never met her.

Luna was the first to regain use of her words. "Mom, Ida died over forty years ago."

Logan had moved a little closer to me. He might be totally freaked out by all of us, but it seemed I was the safest option. He shook his head. "Cats don't live that long."

My mom raised a thin brow at him. "*Mundane* cats

don't live that long." She shifted her attention to me. "This cat has been waiting for you for a very long time, my dear. I wonder if you inherited some of my sister's gifts."

"That's not possible," I argued, "I've never been able to channel."

Luna and Callie's lips twisted with identical expressions of worry. None of us had to say what we were thinking. Ida had been able to channel. She could take in energies, either from the dead or other beings, and let them speak through her mouth. The ability had driven her mad, and had resulted in her death.

Logan cleared his throat. "Sorry to interrupt, but maybe we should talk about Neil Howard's ghost."

My mom gave him a brilliant smile. She was like that, her mood could either light up a room, or cast everyone in darkness. "My, how readily accepting you are of our world. That will save us some time." She stepped back near the couch so she could look at all of us. "We'll need to go to Neil's grave at the witching hour. The binding ritual is relatively simple, but we'll need to be prepared if whatever is controlling the ghost shows up." Her dark eyes fell on me. "This thing is after you, Addy. We need to find out why, because even if we get rid of Neil's ghost, it could still send others."

I swallowed the lump in my throat. I might have had my issues with my mother, but I was glad she had come.

"Just tell me what I need to do. I have a familiar now, I'm strong enough to help."

Her smile held too many secrets, things she kept from us all. "I imagine you are. Now let's get to work. We have much to prepare."

Logan stepped close to me as my mom started discussing things with my sisters. "What is channeling?" he whispered. "You and your sisters seemed upset about it."

I knelt and lifted Spooky off the floor, standing with him cradled in my arms. Could he really be the same cat Ida had? "It's a dangerous gift, probably more of a curse. When you can channel spirits, they tend to haunt you, wanting another chance at life."

"Do you think that's why this," he hesitated, lifting a hand as he grasped for the right word, "*thing* is after you?"

I shivered at the thought. "I don't think so. I've never actually been able to channel. The only thing me and my mom's sister have in common is this cat."

He looked down at the cat in my arms. "I am taking a lot on faith here, but I can't quite bring myself to believe that this cat is over forty years old."

I gave Spooky a light squeeze. "There are a lot of strange things in this world, detective. Just because you don't believe in them, doesn't mean they're not real."

"Are you trying to tell me *the truth is out there*?"

I wrinkled my nose. "I take it I'm Mulder in this situation?"

"Something like that."

We both watched my mom and sisters huddled together. It was always like this, I was the odd woman out. "You're a strange man, detective."

"You should probably start calling me Logan. I think we've gone way beyond regular police work."

I lifted a brow. "Don't tell me you're planning on coming to Neil's grave with us."

His expression went serious as he turned to me. "You're in danger, Addy, and I swore an oath to protect the innocent. What kind of cop would I be if I let you and your family go to that gravesite alone?"

"A smart one. You're a mundane, Logan. You don't understand what we're dealing with."

"Well you have a few hours to explain it to me." When I looked a question at him, he clarified, "Your mom said the witching hour. Some believe that means midnight, while others dispute that it would be 3 AM. Either way, we have a few hours to kill."

My eyes went wide. "Have you been reading up on witches?"

He shrugged. "You started out a suspect, and a lot of people in town claimed you were a witch." The corner of his mouth ticked up. "Not that I believed it at the time, but I did my research just in case you *thought* you were a witch."

"And what do you believe now?"

His back straightened as my mom and sisters broke their huddle and turned toward us. "I think I'd just like to get through this night," he muttered, "and figure it all out come morning."

It was a sound plan, and exactly what I had been thinking. "Well then here's hoping we all live to see the sunrise."

He looked to my family, then to me. "Was that supposed to be comforting?"

"No," we all said in unison.

Logan sighed. "I didn't think so."

CHAPTER FOURTEEN

We arrived at Neil's grave shortly before midnight. I had explained to Logan that the witching hour wasn't so much an hour as a window of time. Any time between midnight and 3 AM would do. That was when the veil was thinnest, and our powers were at their peak.

Spooky trotted near my feet as my boots slid through the damp grass. I could sense dark energy all around, concentrated at a single spot not far off. That had to be the location of Neil's fresh grave.

Luna carried a satchel with the candles, herbs, and sea salt needed for the ritual. She had picked up her familiar, a raven named Ollie, from her house. It had provided me a bit of amusement watching Logan pretending not to glance at the raven perched on her shoulder.

Callie's familiar, a gecko named Sir Vincent, was less obvious riding in her little fanny pack.

My mom had never possessed a familiar as long as I'd been alive, and she never shared why that was. She was a powerful witch, powerful enough to attract a magical animal companion to enhance her magic, but she never tried. It was just one of the many mysteries about my mother.

We reached the grave. The marker was a simple rectangular plaque in the grass. Passing through the dark magic surrounding the grave was like passing through quicksand.

I glanced over my shoulder at Logan. "You may want to step back for this part."

He took a few steps away toward an older gravestone. "Is this good?"

"Sure." I wondered if he would sense a bit of the ritual standing as close as he was. It might spook him a little, but it wouldn't harm him since he was among the living.

Luna walked around the grave with the sea salt, forming a white oval. The salt was meant to keep the spirit contained while the binding ritual took place. She dusted her hands, then started placing white pillar candles around the outer edge of the oval.

Callie and my mom stood close together, watching

on silently. We all knew what to do, but my mom would be the guide to bind our magic together.

Spooky pressed against my leg. *Danger*. The word echoed through my mind.

"Something's wrong," I blurted.

My sisters glanced around, but my mom's attention remained on the grave. A small green light formed near the headstone, pulsing and growing larger.

My mom's eyes darted to Luna. "Light the candles, *now*." She took Callie's hand. "Start chanting."

I hurried over, taking Callie's other hand. We started chanting old words taught to us as soon as we could talk, mostly Latin with a few other near-dead languages thrown in. I forced my words through my tightened throat.

Luna finished lighting the candles, then tossed herbs over the flames before running to take my mom's other hand.

The green light grew, and with it the presence of dark magic. I didn't dare take my eyes off the grave to look for Logan.

Spooky pressed against my calf. The moment he touched me, my magic seemed to flow more freely.

Callie's voice came out high and strained, "It's not working!"

"That's because that isn't Neil's ghost," my mom snapped.

As if he'd heard his name, Neil's ghost formed beyond the green light. He was hardly visible, still weakened by what we'd done to him at my house.

He hovered over his grave, pointing a finger at me, through the light. "Murderer!" he howled.

I squeezed Callie's sweaty palm. "Who told you that!"

"Murderer!" His spectral form expanded, growing until it pushed against the salt circle.

The green light swirled large enough to look like a star brought down to earth, then shot into Neil's chest.

"It's giving him power," my mom's words cut through my sisters' chants. "He's going to break the circle."

Neil became more solid, but impossibly large, filled with a pulsing green glow. He pressed his hands against the invisible barrier of the salt circle. The magic stretched like a rubber band in my mind.

Channel him, a voice went through my thoughts.

I glanced down at Spooky to find him staring up at me.

Channel him, the voice said again.

"I don't know how," I gasped.

The magic of the salt circle broke with an audible *pop*. Neil's ghost radiated with green light, growing ever larger to loom before us.

Do it! The voice echoed in my ears, though I knew it was just in my mind.

"Curse it all," I growled, pulling my hand free from Callie's.

I ignored my sisters' shouts and jumped directly into the ghost. My body went ice cold. I collapsed to the ground, and it took every ounce of effort just to roll myself over. The green light and the dark magic presence were gone. I couldn't sense it anymore.

But I could still sense Neil's ghost. I could sense it because it was inside of me.

My body sat up of its own volition, looking at my sisters and mom with seething rage. Logan was just a few steps behind them. He had his gun out, but didn't seem to know where to point it.

Words spilled out of my mouth, directed at me. "Let me go, witch."

Callie gasped. "What's happening?"

Luna stared at me, but it was my mom who answered, "She channeled the ghost. All we can do is wait and find out who is stronger."

I staggered to my feet, or I guess Neil staggered to my feet. I wasn't in charge anymore. "Let me go!" My head whipped toward Logan, noticing his gun. "Shoot me." My body shuffled toward him. Neil was controlling my steps, but he was having difficulty. "Shoot me!" They weren't my words. Neil was trying to get me killed.

Wide-eyed, Logan stumbled back, pointing his gun skyward.

My mom stepped between me and him. Her dark eyes seemed to bore into my skull. "You have to fight it, Addy."

"I can't," I gasped, regaining control for just a heartbeat.

I fell to my knees, hunching over. I couldn't feel anything beyond Neil's hatred. He didn't actually know who killed him, he couldn't remember, and he wasn't sure why he thought it was me. He didn't know where the idea had come from. So imbued with dark magic, he'd broken into my house to search for proof.

I warred with his thoughts, wishing I could communicate, but nothing could cut through his anger and confusion. I was losing my hold on my own mind.

Something jumped onto my back, and I distantly realized it was Spooky. Suddenly I could feel the earth beneath my knees, and I could sense my family surrounding me. Spooky brought me back to myself enough to fight.

I pressed my hands over Neil's grave. None of the old words would come to mind, so I'd just have to use my own. "I bind you, Neil Howard. I bind you to your grave. Rest and know peace."

I repeated the words, and my sisters and mother joined in. They huddled around me, linking hands, and together we spoke, "We bind you, Neil Howard. We bind you to your grave. Rest and know peace." We repeated the words over and over, building in power each time.

The magic reached its breaking point. My body lurched forward as a cool white mist spewed out of my mouth. The mist soaked into the ground below me. Suddenly my thoughts were all my own again.

My shoulders shook, and I wasn't sure if I was laughing or crying. Probably a little bit of both. "He's gone."

"Oh thank goddess." Luna fell to her knees and hugged me. Ollie extended his wings from atop her shoulder, struggling to balance himself.

Spooky hopped off my back and came around to rub against my hands.

Callie knelt down beside us, but my mom stayed standing, staring down. "The ghost may be gone, but whatever called it is still out here, watching."

We all glanced around in the darkness, but nothing moved other than Logan walking toward us.

He peered down at me with wide, horror-filled eyes. "What just happened?"

I wondered if I looked as bad as I felt. "Do you really want to know?"

"I'm not sure. Maybe not."

Callie and Luna helped me stand. I tried to walk on my own, but nearly fell, and had to grab back onto them.

"Well that's good, because I'm not sure what I would tell you."

My mom started gathering up the extinguished candles. "We can talk about this at home. You're all coming home with me tonight where you'll be safe."

Part of me wanted to give in and take my mom's protection, but another part of me had just channeled and banished a ghost. "I'm taking Spooky to my home tonight. The rest of you can do what you want."

My mom stood with the candles in her arms. "You don't know what you're dealing with, Adelaide. My sister—"

"But I'm not your sister," I interrupted. "I need to figure this out myself."

She watched me for a moment, then nodded.

Callie wrapped her arm around my waist. "Let's get out of here. This graveyard is giving me the creeps."

My sisters helped me stumble back to the car. Ollie was hiding in Luna's hair, and neither sister seemed to want to meet my eyes.

I could tell myself that they were just afraid of the dark magic returning, but I knew that wasn't it. At least, it wasn't all of it.

Tonight, I had channeled a ghost. The power was like a faucet, one no witch could turn off.

At least, that's what I had been told, but it wasn't about to stop me from trying.

CHAPTER FIFTEEN

After one last attempt at convincing me to go home with her, my mom left. I had told Callie and Luna to go too, but they were now both upstairs, getting ready for bed. It seemed we would be having sleepovers until the dark magic was dealt with. Of course, that hadn't stopped them from intentionally giving me a moment alone with Logan.

I wasn't sure I wanted the moment. He waited in the living room while I made tea in the kitchen, which he had finally accepted.

I carried in a little tray with two mugs of chamomile and set them on the coffee table. Every light was on in the house, the normally soft white glow seeming harsh at such an ungodly hour. I took a seat on one of the chairs adjacent the sofa, not sure Logan would want me anywhere near him after what he'd seen.

After a little bit of prodding, he lifted his mug and took a sip. It didn't seem to relax him in the slightest.

I sucked my teeth, debating what to say. "I'm sure you have questions."

He took another sip of tea. Dark circles marred his deep brown eyes, seeming to fit with his wrinkled slacks and unbuttoned collar. He hung his head a little lower. "Still trying to formulate them."

I watched him while I waited. Honestly, I was shocked he hadn't run away after seeing Neil's ghost the first time. That he hadn't run from the graveyard meant he was either brave or stupid, probably a bit of both.

He took a deep inhale. "So Neil's ghost, it's gone?"

"Yes, but just the ghost, not whoever or whatever sent it after me to begin with."

He set his half-full mug back on the table. "Do you think whatever sent Neil's ghost after you is also what actually killed him?"

I let out a breath of relief. He still believed I wasn't the murderer, even after all he had seen. He had watched me channel a ghost, and he still believed I was one of the good guys . . . or at least not one of the bad guys. "Maybe, but I'm not entirely sure. I've been able to sense the dark magic whenever it's near, but when that truck tried to hit us, I didn't sense anything. I think the driver was a mundane. Come to think of it, I didn't sense the dark magic when I found Neil's body either. I think someone else killed him, and the dark magic is just taking advantage of a confused ghost."

He finally met my eyes, though it seemed to take effort. "So we still have no idea who killed him?"

I shrugged. "Nope, though my money is on Blake Monroe. Have you managed to find him yet?"

He shook his head, seeming to relax now that the conversation was back on normal police business. "We're still looking. Once I get Mary's information from your veterinarian friend tomorrow, I'll ask her about him."

"She was going to call him, so he won't have any information from her until the afternoon. Although, she did mention Tammy said she could wait tables at the tavern, so you might be able to find her information there."

His expression turned thoughtful. "I'll question Tammy first thing then." He stood. "I should probably get going."

I stood and walked him to the door. The whole conversation had been a lot less painful than I had been expecting. Of course, he'd avoided asking me much.

With his hand on the knob, he turned back to me. "Will you be safe here tonight? I could call an officer back to watch your house."

I leaned back, a bit surprised by his concern. "My sisters are just upstairs. I'll be fine."

"Your sisters were there with you tonight too, and they didn't seem to be much help."

My gut clenched, because he was right. As much as my sisters would try to protect me, I had a creeping feeling that I was on my own.

Spooky came into the living room and hopped on the couch, watching us. Maybe I wasn't entirely alone. I was pretty sure he was the one who had spoken into my mind and told me what to do with Neil's ghost. Maybe he could tell me what to do about the dark magic too.

With a sigh, I turned back to the detective. "I'm afraid I won't be entirely safe anywhere, but there's nothing you can do about that. I think for now we just need to focus on solving the murder, and hope that everything else falls into place."

He opened the door. "You leave that part to me, just focus on staying safe."

I watched him as he stepped outside. I almost didn't want to bring it up, but— "Hey Logan?"

He turned back to me, framed in the light of my front drive.

"You know the whole thing about me being a witch? Do you think you could not tell anyone? Being out in the open hasn't historically worked out well for us."

The corner of his lip ticked up. "I think I can leave that part out of my investigation report. I should probably leave out the ghost too."

I smiled. "Thanks, I'll see you later."

I watched him walk down the drive and get in his car before I shut my front door. Wouldn't do to have some dark magical force swooping in the moment I turned my back.

Once the sound of his engine receded in the distance, I shut and locked the door, turning as my sisters came down the stairs.

Callie walked around the couch and leaned her butt against the arm. "So is he freaked out?"

I shrugged. "A little, but at least he's not gathering townspeople to burn us at the stake."

Luna remained standing by the stairs, looking back and forth between us. "We need to figure out what to do about that dark magic," she eyed me pointedly, "and about you being able to channel. How did you know what to do?"

I walked over to the couch and sat, taking up my cooling mug of tea. "I think Spooky told me. Well, he told me to channel the ghost. The jumping in was my idea."

Luna walked around Callie's outstretched legs to sit beside me. "So do we believe mom then? Was he Ida's familiar?"

The cat jumped up on the coffee table, and we all turned to stare at him.

"But if that's true," I began, "why did he just come to me now? I was born seven or eight years after Ida died."

Luna patted my leg. "Maybe you weren't ready."

I leaned forward, bracing my elbows on my knees to hide my frown. Why wouldn't I have been ready? Both of my sisters got their first familiars when they were teenagers. Although, their animals weren't like mine. They might live a little longer than normal, but they didn't live over forty years.

The cat blinked back at me, offering no explanations.

I sighed. "I should get some rest while I still can. I need to open the cafe in the morning."

Luna sat bolt upright. "You can't possibly be thinking of going to work in the morning. Something powerful is out for your blood."

"And that's not going to change whether I'm here or there." I stood. "I can't hide from this thing. All I can do is try to figure out who killed Neil, and hope that it's connected."

I walked around the sofa toward the stairs. Spooky hopped up and followed at my heels. I paused with my hand on the banister. "I'll see you both in the morning. I appreciate you being here."

Callie tilted her head back to look at me. "Love you, sis. I don't care that you're a scary channeler now, you're still our Adelaide."

I blew her a kiss and walked up the stairs with

Spooky following close behind. While I appreciated Callie's sentiment, I wasn't sure I could agree. I wasn't just the same old Adelaide anymore.

I had channeled a ghost. It was an ill omen for any witch. Now that the gates were open, other spirits would notice. Some would simply want help, but others would try to take me over for another chance at life.

I could only hope that Spooky had waited for me for a reason, and that he knew how to keep me from the same fate Ida suffered. Of course, with an old dark magic and a mundane murderer after my blood, I might not survive long enough for it to be an issue.

CHAPTER SIXTEEN

The next morning I took Spooky to work with me. I needed to open the cafe, but I wasn't too keen on being without him. I had gotten dressed in a long-sleeved black blouse, topped by a black coat, the color befitting my mood. Normally I avoided too much black since most of the town folk already thought I was a witch, but today I was beyond caring.

Spooky trotted at my side down Mueller Street, then followed me as I took a right and eventually headed past Golden Dollar Pawn. Just as I passed the store front, my steps halted, then I took a few steps back. The sign in the window was flipped to *Open*.

Blake Monroe stood behind the counter within.

It only took me a second to consider my options, then I was opening the door and heading inside, leaving room for Spooky to follow. I waited for a strange reaction as I walked up to the counter. If Blake was the murderer, he could also be the person who tried to run me and Logan over.

He was either a very good actor, or he didn't know anything. He smiled. "How can I help you?"

I scanned the objects beneath the glass countertop, feigning interest. "Oh, just a little early for work, I figured I'd take a browse." I glanced up at him with mild curiosity. "You were out of town." I took in his clean, blue button up shirt, and neatly combed blond hair. He didn't look like a man with worries.

He winced at my question. "Yeah, a bit of a bad break up, I decided to go camping for a few days."

"A break up?" I inquired, hoping he wouldn't think I was interested. Then again, him thinking I was flirting might help.

He turned away and started arranging stuff on the shelves mounted in the back wall. "Yeah, you know the story, girl left me for another guy."

I was glad his back was to me, or else he would have caught my sudden interest. Mary hadn't mentioned there being someone else involved in Blake becoming her ex. "That's the worst. Did you know the guy?"

He took down a box of objects, clanking metal pieces together within. For a moment I worried he had a gun, then he set the box down, revealing some jewelry and watches. "Maybe you'll be interested in some of these, and yeah, I knew the guy. We used to be friends until she started working for him."

I dropped the watch I had lifted to inspect. "Oh! Excuse me. I haven't had enough coffee this morning."

He leaned one hand against the counter. "Speaking of coffee, maybe I'll come by your cafe one of these days."

Was he threatening me? I looked up, and he gave me a crooked but charming smile. Ah, definitely not threatening.

I stepped away from the counter, pulling my cell phone out of my back pocket. "Oops, killed a little bit too much time. I better go." I rushed toward the door.

"Don't forget your cat!" he called after me, but Spooky was already at my heels following me outside.

I turned on the sidewalk as a car pulled up to the curb, quickly recognizing it as Logan's.

He shut off the engine and stepped out, narrowing his eyes at me. He still looked a little tired from last night, though his casual suit was freshly pressed.

I lifted my hands in surrender before he could speak. "I was just browsing, not asking any questions."

Logan stepped up on the sidewalk, then moved close to me. He lowered his voice, "Addy, he could be a murderer. He could be the person who tried to hit you."

I wrinkled my nose. "More like hit *on* me, and I learned something interesting. Blake claims Mary left him for her boss. Her boss was Neil."

He moved closer to me, bringing with him the smell of fresh soap and shaving cream, no aftershave or cologne. "That makes him seem *more* like a murderer, not less, and you were just alone in his shop with him."

"He just got back to town," I whispered. "I'm pretty sure he doesn't even know Neil is dead, let alone who killed him." Spooky leaned against my leg, reminding me I had someplace I needed to be. I took a step back. "I'm late to open the cafe, I need to go. The regulars will be waiting."

Logan swiped a hand over his face, shaking his head. "I would appreciate it if you stayed inside the cafe until closing, I can give you a ride home when you're done."

I shrugged. "Sure, if that would make you feel better." Inside, I was sighing with relief. I had been worried that after last night, Logan would avoid me, effectively cutting me out of the investigation.

I waved goodbye, leaving him to question Blake, though I really didn't think he would learn anything new. I believed that Blake had just been out camping, and that's why the cops hadn't been able to find him. So who did that leave on my suspect list? Mary? Sasha? Or maybe there was someone else we didn't know about. Someone else who was in love with Mary, and wanted Neil out of the way.

I still had a lot of questions, good thing I knew just who to ask.

FAMILIAR SPIRITS

I CALLED Max from my office on my lunch break. "Have you heard from Mary yet?"

"Who is this?" he asked sarcastically.

"The pope. Have you heard from her?"

"Addy," he sighed, "someone tried to run you over. Are you sure you want to keep looking into this?"

"I'm in too deep, Max. And I just want to ask her a few questions."

He sighed again. "All right, she called, and I visited Ike this morning. He insisted on taking care of Neil's debt himself. He seems to think he's personally responsible for all the trouble Neil caused. I'm walking over to drop a check off to Mary in a few minutes."

"Give me the address, I'll meet you there."

"I don't think so. I'll meet you at the cafe and we'll go together. Do you have someone to cover for you?"

"Evie is here," I explained, "but just for a few hours."

"It shouldn't take long, she doesn't live far from you."

"I'll wait for you at the cafe then, see you soon."

He said goodbye, then hung up.

I put my phone back in my pocket as I debated how to approach things with Mary. Did I tell her that I knew she had been dating Neil? Or did I dance around it and see what she might admit?

Spooky sat on my desk, watching me.

Maybe he could take a look around Mary's house while I talked to her. I hoped she liked cats.

I went back out into the cafe with Spooky, thinking I could make Max a coffee as a thank you, but Francis Brookes spotted me and beckoned me over to her table. She and Elmer must have come back while I was calling Max.

Elmer smiled and straightened his spectacles as I approached.

"Back for your lunchtime fix?" I asked.

He lifted his cup with a nod, though I knew it would only contain decaf. Neither he nor his wife would sleep at night if they had caffeine after noon.

Francis pointed to the free chair. "Sit, Addy, we need to talk."

Her tone made my pulse race. Had she heard I was sticking my nose into a murder investigation? Or had Logan lied about keeping quiet? Did she know I was an actual witch?

Spooky hopped up into my lap as soon as I sat.

Francis gave me a brilliant smile, wrinkling every line in her face, and there were a lot of them. "I'm told you've been spending some time with the handsome veterinarian. I was worried with your new pet," she gestured to Spooky in my lap, "you'd given up on men entirely."

I felt so silly I could've smacked myself. Of course Francis was only thinking about romance. It was her favorite genre after mysteries. "Max and I are just friends, Francis."

She tilted her head. "But you could become more? You're not getting any younger, Addy."

I kept a smile on my face. I would tolerate such comments from few people, and Francis was one of them. "We'll see, Francis. But for now, just friends."

"Just friends, eh?" Elmer was looking out the front window.

Max reached the door, spotted me, then gave a little wave. So much for making him a coffee, there wasn't time now. Or maybe there was, but I didn't want to use it. I was anxious to ask Mary more questions.

I stood. "If you'll both excuse me, I have somewhere to be."

Francis winked at me. "I'll just bet you do."

I laughed as I headed out the door, waving bye to Evie as I went. I held the door open for Spooky, then turned to face Max. His hair was a little more mussed than usual, and there were bags beneath his brown eyes. "Did you have a rough night?"

He looked down at his shoes. "If we're being honest, I was a little worried about you. I wanted to make sure you got home safe, but I wasn't sure if it was my place to call."

Feeling eyes on me, I glanced through the front window. Francis was staring intently.

I grabbed Max's arm to get him walking. "You could've called, but I got home just fine. Totally uneventful night." *And pigs can fly,* I added silently.

"That's good to hear. Was the detective too upset with you?"

I glanced at him, wondering about his interest on the subject. "I think the detective is in a constant state of upset, but no, he wasn't too mad. After all, I didn't seek Mary out, she came to us."

"Was he interested in what you learned from her?"

I hopped over a crack in the sidewalk, my motion echoed by Spooky. "Yes, actually. He was going to call you today to get her information so he could question her."

Max stopped walking, then turned to face me. "Addy, if the police want to question her, we shouldn't go over there. You should call the detective and give him her address."

I rolled my eyes. "Logan questioned Blake earlier, I'm sure he already has the address. He may even be there now."

He watched me for a moment. "We'll drop the check off, that's it."

"Of course." Once I knew where Mary lived, I could always go back.

We started walking again with Max giving me occasional directions. Spooky walked a few steps ahead, glancing back to make sure we weren't taking any turns. Max was right, she did live near me. We even passed the spot where Neil had been murdered on the way.

Max stopped in front of a mailbox shaped like a little house and checked his phone, then looked at the address on the box. "This is it, and remember, we're just dropping off the check."

I glanced at the house. There was nothing remarkable about it, just a plain little house with tan paint and a white picket fence. "Of course."

We walked up the narrow driveway together, then took the stepping stones cutting across the grass to the front door. Max knocked, and we waited.

Mary opened the door. She was wearing another crimson blouse, this one long-sleeved and cut low on her chest. She obviously knew the color looked spectacular on her. Her dark hair framed her thin face, but did nothing to conceal the sudden irritation as her eyes landed on me.

Her attention darted back to Max. "I didn't realize you were bringing someone along."

"I hope you don't mind." He took his wallet out of his back pocket and withdrew the check. "I figured it would be alright since I was just dropping this off." He handed it to her.

She snatched it with well-manicured fingers. "Well you might as well still come in. I figured since you were on your lunch break, I would make you something to eat."

I was glad she was watching Max so closely, so she didn't see my eyebrows shoot up.

He turned to me, obviously too polite to say no. Or maybe he didn't want to say no, and I was misreading everything.

"Sure," I said with a smile. I felt bad for Max's discomfort, but I wasn't about to pass up an opportunity to see inside her house.

Her smile was more of a grimace. She looked down at Spooky sitting by my feet. "The cat will have to stay outside. I'm allergic."

Go, a voice spoke into my head, making me jump. I didn't hide my surprise quickly enough.

Mary's upper lip lifted slightly as she looked down her nose at me. "Are you alright?"

I forced a smile. Oh boy, another person who thought I was a nut. Though maybe this time it could work to my advantage. "I'm fine, I just thought I saw a spider. Spooky can wait out here."

Mary's eyes narrowed, but she opened the door wide and stepped aside.

Max gave me a look only I could see as I entered. A look which said he had clearly been betrayed when I accepted her invitation.

I gave him a little salute, then walked into the living

room. The carpets were a pale cream that wouldn't have lasted a month in my house. My white couch was challenge enough. Every wooden surface was clean and gleaming. The couch had a plastic cover over it.

"Nice place," I said as Max came to stand at my back.

Mary shut the door, then walked past us, taking a moment to put the check in her purse where it was hanging from a hook on the wall. "Lunch is in the kitchen."

I was the first to follow her, so I got to see the neatly arranged lunch for two before she haphazardly tossed another place setting and glass onto the table.

I couldn't help but stare at the tray of sandwiches. She had cut off the crusts. A glass bottle of fancy sparkling water dripped condensation onto the white tablecloth.

She had planned a romantic lunch for her and Max, which was more than odd, since they didn't know each other.

We all sat, and an awkward silence ensued.

"Well?" Mary said expectantly. "Dig in."

I took a sandwich, though I didn't really want one, glancing around her kitchen. Though she had just prepared lunch, every countertop was freshly wiped and there were no dishes in the sink. It was the third meticulously clean house I'd visited in that number of days. Maybe I just had low standards, but I didn't think so.

I took a bite of the sandwich, assuming it wasn't poison since she was trying to seduce Max, not kill him. At least I hoped. The sandwich was turkey and cheese, and was actually pretty good.

"So have you started working at the tavern yet?" I asked Mary.

Her frown softened. "Not yet, Tammy has a pretty rigorous process for new employees."

"Rigorous?"

She huffed. "Two forms of ID. How many people carry around two forms of ID? I had to request a new copy of my birth certificate." She looked to Max, dismissing me. "How was Ike? I only met him a time or two, but he must have been devastated about his son."

Max had put a sandwich on his plate, but hadn't tried it yet. "Yeah, he's pretty torn up about it, and he's upset that the police haven't found the killer yet. He thinks it was one of Neil's business schemes gone wrong."

She shrugged. "I'm sure it's only a matter of time. They have to have some suspects by now. I do hope they have questioned Desmond."

I dropped my sandwich on my plate at her words, then covered my surprise by reaching for the bottle of sparkling water. I poured some into the glass she had put down with my place setting. "Do you really think

Desmond knows something about what happened to Neil?"

She pursed her lips. "Of course he does. They were brothers, and they were always scheming together. If anyone knows who killed Neil, it's Desmond. Or maybe he even did it himself."

My eyes widened. She sure had come a long way from casually mentioning an argument before, to blatantly accusing Desmond now.

"Did you tell all of this to the police?" Max asked.

She looked genuinely shocked. "Of course I did. I may not have particularly cared for Neil, but I want his murder solved."

Suuuure, I thought.

She gave me a long look. "I asked Tammy about you. She said you own that little cafe, and that you and Neil didn't really know each other. I had assumed you were one of his lovers for you to take such interest in his murder."

I chose to ignore her derisive tone when speaking of my cafe, which was easy to do with my brain struggling to catch up with her blatant accusation. "Definitely not a lover," I assured her. I could tell she was waiting for further explanation. "Honestly, he had my phone number in his pocket when he died. I was hoping to figure out why that was?" I said it like it was a question.

She had been his secretary after all, and the handwriting had been feminine.

She looked to Max, then back to me. "How should I know? I didn't even know you existed until yesterday."

I knew it was a lie, at least in part. I had seen her around town, so it stood to reason she at least vaguely knew who I was. It made me wonder if she had been the one to write down my phone number, though I couldn't for the life of me figure out why.

"We should get going," Max interjected. "I told my employee I wouldn't be gone long."

Had he realized I was trying to figure out how to ask her about her relationship with Neil? I stuffed the rest of my sandwich into my mouth before I could say anything out loud, then swallowed it in a painful gulp.

She looked to Max. "Surely you could stay a little longer."

He stood, leaving his half-finished sandwich on his plate. "I have an appointment soon too, I'm sorry. But thank you for the lovely lunch."

She seemed frozen for a moment, then nodded. "I'll show you out then."

The short walk to the front door seemed to take a million years. Only once we were alone and walking down the driveway did my shoulders relax.

"What happened to not questioning her?" Max muttered.

I shrugged. "Opportunity knocked, and I answered." I stopped where Spooky was waiting for us next to the mailbox.

Max snorted at my answer, then looked down. "That's a well-behaved cat."

"You have no idea." I glanced over my shoulder as we started down the sidewalk, just to make sure Mary wasn't watching, then turned my full attention to Max. "Did it seem a bit odd how she was talking about Desmond?"

"I was thinking the same thing. She was the one who pointed us there to begin with. I assumed Desmond was lying about not seeing Neil, but now I wonder if Mary is the one lying."

I glanced over my shoulder again, though her house was out of view. "You mean like she's setting Desmond up?"

He shrugged one shoulder. "Maybe. Something isn't adding up. Did you notice how upset she was that Tammy wanted two forms of ID?"

"And Neil was paying her under the table. Who would take an under the table job that paid below minimum wage?"

Max stopped walking to look at me. "Someone trying to hide who they are. We should call the detective."

I glanced back again, feeling uneasy. Spooky stopped and glanced back with me. "Let's get back to the cafe first. I've got the creeps."

Max shivered. "You and me both."

As we started walking again, I considered what we'd learned. Mary wasn't who she said she was, and she wanted Neil's brother to go down for his murder. She also had a house as meticulously clean as Desmond's. I'd thought Sasha had been the one to clean for him, but maybe I was wrong.

But who would clean someone's house, then accuse them of murder? Blake thought Mary left him for Neil, but maybe he was mistaken. Maybe she left him for Desmond. And maybe Desmond had ended things, and now Mary was trying to set him up for murder.

But did that mean Mary had killed Neil? Maybe, but we had no proof, nor any real motive. Either way, I would tell Logan what we had learned, and I would take the lecture he would give me for questioning another suspect.

Eventually we got back to the cafe, and I realized I'd be getting that lecture sooner than expected. Logan was waiting for me inside.

CHAPTER SEVENTEEN

"Speak of the devil," Max said, spotting Logan the same time I did. "I guess this saves us a call."

Logan headed our way like a tall, dark, angry cloud. As he opened the door, Spooky rushed in, clearly not wanting to be a part of the situation. Logan stepped outside, facing us on the sidewalk. His gaze settled on me. "Where have you been?"

I put my hands on my hips. "Now how is that any of your business?"

"It's my business, because I went to your friend's clinic to get Mary's info," he gestured to Max. "His secretary said he was dropping a check off to someone, then I come to the cafe to find you missing, with your employee not knowing where you went."

I furrowed my brow, moving aside as a couple walked past us on the sidewalk. "Well if you already guessed that we had gone to Mary's, why ask me where I've been? And why not just get Mary's information from Blake?"

He sighed. "I figured I'd give you a chance to make up an excuse, and I didn't want Blake calling Mary ahead of time to let her know I was coming. We didn't have enough on him to take him to the station, and his story checks out. He was sold a camping permit and witnesses placed him several times at the country market buying bait."

I glanced at Max. "Do you want to tell him, or should I?"

Max raised his hands, palms up. "You're the one that accepted her invitation inside, I'll let you tell."

I smirked. "Traitor."

"If you two are quite through," Logan interjected, "we can talk in my car."

Feeling a bit like a scorned teenager who stayed out too late, I followed Logan and Max to Logan's car parked just a few spots away. I tried to beat Max to the backseat, but he was faster and I ended up in the passenger seat next to Logan.

"All right, start talking," Logan ordered.

We told him our suspicions about Mary, starting with her not wanting to provide ID to Tammy and ending with her trying to set up Desmond.

Logan's mood seemed even sourer by the time we finished.

"Let me guess, you already knew all of this?" I asked.

"No, I didn't, and it's a little irritating that the person I've repeatedly ordered to stay off my case has discovered more information than I have."

I grinned. "Aw, I done good."

He angled his body so he could look at both me and Max. "You also entered the house of a potential murderer. I will keep everything you've told me in mind when I question Mary, but from now on, stay out of it."

I lifted my hands in surrender. "Alright, alright, but if Mary's the murderer, just don't let her get away."

"I'll try not to," he said caustically. He looked to Max. "I'd like a moment alone with Ms. O'Shea, if you don't mind."

"Of course," he said, then patted my shoulder. "I have to head back to the clinic, I'll call you later."

I flashed him a smile. "Sounds good."

My smile wilted once I was left alone with Logan. I wasn't sure what he would need to say to me alone. We had already told him everything we learned about Mary.

He watched me for a long moment before speaking. He no longer looked angry, more . . . conflicted. "About the other night, what happened in the graveyard—" he hesitated.

Ah, of course. I chewed my lower lip, not sure what to say. "Go on."

"Has anything else happened? Are you still in danger?"

I forced a smile, then lied through my teeth. "I think the worst of the danger with that has passed."

His eyes narrowed, and I got the sensation he could see right through to my thoughts. "You would tell me if anything else happened, right? I know I don't know much about your world, but I still might be able to help."

"I appreciate the sentiment, but you're better off forgetting everything you saw. Your job is to deal with mundane bad guys. You are not obligated to deal with anything else."

His jaw went a little slack. "I wasn't asking because I feel obligated."

I shrugged, feeling uncomfortable. He was the first mortal who knew I was an actual witch, and I wasn't quite sure how to deal with it. "Well either way I'm fine, and I'll be careful. You just focus on Mary." I reached for the door handle.

"I'm not sure how long things will take with Mary. Can someone walk you home tonight?"

I hesitated with my hand on the handle. If I said no, would he make sure he was available? Did I want him to? "I'm sure one of my sisters will come meet me." I opened the door a crack. "And thanks for your concern. It's surprising, but also nice that you're not running for the hills."

I opened the door and got out before he could say anything else. He had a murder to solve, I had a cafe to run, and that's all there was to it.

I walked into the cafe to find Spooky sitting in Sophie's lap on the sofa. Richie, Elmer, and Francis were with her. I was surprised about the latter two, since I'd seen them before I left with Max. They had been hanging around practically all day.

Richie waved me over.

I caught Evie's attention behind the counter to see if she needed anything, but she gave me a thumbs up. I had some time before she needed to leave.

I walked over to Richie. "What's up?"

He ran a hand over his slicked-back black hair, glancing to Sophie, who quickly looked down at the cat in her lap and twirled a finger through her blonde ponytail.

I looked to Francis and Elmer, knowing one of them would surely spit it out. "All right you guys, what's going on? This better not be about Max."

Richie leaned forward and whispered, "Are you trying to solve Neil Howard's murder?"

I grabbed a nearby chair, spinning it around and placing it to face Richie and the others. I sat down and lowered my voice. "What are you talking about?"

Richie shrugged, crinkling his leather jacket. "Well, that detective keeps coming around, and Blake Monroe came in a few minutes ago looking for you. He said you were asking a bunch of questions right before the police came to question him."

I pursed my lips, trying to think of a good excuse.

"Sophie will know if you lie," Francis warned. "She can always tell."

Well that was news to me. I looked to Sophie, who was blushing furiously.

"It's true," Richie said, "so you better just tell us. Maybe we can help."

I glanced around the mostly empty cafe. The nearest customer was an elderly man browsing the used books. He wasn't close enough to hear us.

I sighed, turning back to the group. "Alright, but none of you breathe a word of this to anyone. I'm only telling you because I'm pretty sure the murderer is about to be arrested."

Sophie's hand froze mid-motion petting Spooky. "Really?"

"Really." I went on to tell them details I didn't think would be dangerous. I glossed over a lot, just in case we were wrong and Mary wasn't the murderer. I also left out her identity.

"Wow, trying to set up the brother," Richie

commented. "You know, my cousin lives next to Desmond. I've met him a few times. He's a nice guy."

I leaned forward in my seat. "You didn't ever happen to see a woman going over there, did you? Maybe one with dark hair?"

He thought about it. "I did see someone one time, but I only saw her from behind. She was blonde though."

"Why is that important?" Elmer asked.

I almost didn't hear him. A blonde woman had gone to visit Desmond. Could it be . . . I stood. "I'll have to explain later. I need to check something out."

"You be careful, Addy," Francis lectured.

I gave her a little salute. "Always am."

Spooky hopped off Sophie's lap as I put my chair back in place, then headed toward Evie.

She wiped down the counter, giving me a knowing look. "You have one more hour before I have to pick up Sedona."

I grinned. She knew me too well. "I'll try to be quick, but if I'm not back in time just go ahead and close up."

"Will do, boss, as long as you let me know which handsome man you're rushing off to meet."

I rolled my eyes, then scooped Spooky up and headed for the door. I only knew of one blonde who might be visiting Desmond, and I intended to find out why.

CHAPTER EIGHTEEN

The sky was heavy with rain as I pulled up to Sasha's house. During my walk home to pick up the car, then my drive to Sasha's, I had halfway talked myself out of my suspicions. Desmond was her brother-in-law, it wasn't *that* weird that she was visiting him, if it was even her.

I looked to Spooky sitting in the passenger seat. "What do you think, bad idea?"

"Meow?"

With a sigh I unbuckled my seatbelt. "Doesn't hurt to ask, I guess," I muttered.

Spooky hopped out of the car after me and we both walked up the driveway, passing Sasha's little sedan. I was surprised she hadn't gone back to work yet, or maybe she had employees to run the boutique for her.

I knocked, then waited.

Then I waited some more.

I knocked one more time, no longer expecting an answer. After a few more moments of silence, I walked over to the nearest window and peered inside, but the drapes were drawn. All I could see were shadows.

I smell blood, a voice whispered in my mind.

I looked down at Spooky, my heart suddenly thundering in my chest. "Are you sure?" I whispered.

Get inside.

I was glad I didn't sense any dark magic, or I might not have been brave enough to go in alone. But if Spooky smelled blood, Sasha might be hurt, and she might need my help.

I ran back to the front door and tried the knob, but it was locked, then I ran around back, hopping the small picket fence. Sasha's freshly mowed yard was as clean as her house, but I only caught a brief glimpse of it as I ran toward the back door. My breath whooshed out as someone in a black hoodie ran out right in front of me. He seemed male, but that was all I could tell with his hood pulled up as he kept running.

I almost gave chase, but Spooky warned, *Get inside.* The person fleeing the scene had already jumped the back fence by the time I made my decision and ran toward the open back door. I stepped inside, looking around. I was in her laundry room. There was another closed door leading inside.

I heard Spooky's claws on the linoleum behind me as I went to the next door. I grabbed a hammer from the nearby shelf just in case, then slowly opened the door and peeked inside.

The first thing I spotted was Sasha's blonde hair on the carpet, just visible around the corner of the couch. Throwing caution to the wind, I ran and knelt beside her. I couldn't tell if she was asleep or dead, but there was a bleeding wound by her hairline surrounded by a swollen purple bruise.

"Crap," I muttered, pulling my phone out of my pocket with one hand while checking her pulse with the other.

I didn't realize until the time Logan answered that I should have called 911, but he was the first person I had thought to contact.

"Sasha was attacked," I said, interrupting him asking me what was wrong. "I'm at her house now. She has a head wound, but she's still breathing."

"I'm on my way now, I'll call an ambulance. Hang tight."

I glanced around the quiet house, trusting Spooky to warn me if anyone was still around. "I'll be here, just hurry."

I hung up the phone, then looked down at Sasha, wondering who would want to hurt her. The person I'd seen fleeing was of moderate height, and on second thought, maybe it had been a tall woman rather than a short man. I didn't get a good enough look to tell.

All I knew was that I had interrupted what that person was doing. If I hadn't knocked on Sasha's door, would they have killed her?

I still didn't sense any dark magic, which meant her attacker was a mundane. I held Sasha's limp hand and waited. I guessed I could cross her back off the suspect list, because I was pretty sure Neil's murderer had just gotten away.

IT WAS POURING rain by the time Logan arrived, just ahead of the paramedics. I'd had the wherewithal to unlock the front door for him, and he came bursting in, trailed by a gust of icy air and raindrops. He pulled me aside while two female paramedics worked on Sasha.

Water dripped off his hair as he leaned in close. "What happened, Addy? Why are you here?"

I stared at the back of the nearest paramedic. "I just came to ask her a question, but no one was answering even though her car is here. I got worried and went around the back and saw someone running away."

Spooky came up and sat near us on the carpet. I almost debated telling Logan my cat had smelled the blood. I mean, he believed I was a witch, he might believe my cat could speak to me.

The moment passed as the paramedics lifted Sasha up on a stretcher and took her outside.

"Will she be alright?" I asked, though Logan didn't have a way of knowing any more than I did.

I heard a car door shut outside, then two young male officers came into the house.

Logan pressed a hand to the small of my back. "Take your cat and wait in your car, Addy. I'll be right out."

I grabbed Spooky and left Logan to talk with the officers, glad he'd given me an excuse to escape. For some reason, finding Sasha like that had shaken me more than when I found Neil's body. Probably due to the killer fleeing the scene right in front of me.

The ambulance took off as I ran through the rain, clutching the cat to my chest. I threw the door open and we both dove inside, bringing a deluge of water with us.

Spooky and I waited in my car until the windows fogged up. I turned as Logan's distorted form approached the passenger's side. He opened the door, letting in cold air and moisture. Spooky hopped into my lap to make room for him to sit in the passenger seat.

Logan wiped dripping water from his face as he shut the door. His suit was soaked through. "Tell me everything that happened, from the beginning."

I repeated the story, cursing myself for not getting a

better look at the person running away. If I would've reacted more quickly, the case might have been solved.

Logan touched my hand. "You did the right thing. This person already killed once, and just tried to kill again. You would have had no business trying to apprehend them."

I stared out into the rain. "Whoever it was, it wasn't Mary. This person was too tall."

He took his hand back. "I know, I was with Mary when you called. She has an alibi for Neil's murder. I had assumed it wouldn't hold up, but now I'm not so sure."

I shook my head, absentmindedly petting Spooky's wet fur. "None of this makes any sense. Why hurt Sasha?"

"Considering the killer waited so long, I would guess Sasha had figured out who it was. Maybe she confronted them."

I whipped my eyes to him. "Do you think when she wakes up she can tell us who it is?"

He frowned. "*If* she wakes up, Addy. I'll call the hospital to check in on her condition as soon as I make sure you're home safe."

I shook my head. "I need to get back to the cafe."

"Could you please just listen to me for once?" he huffed. "You could have been killed today. And don't forget someone already tried to run us over. If they think you recognized them, they might come after you."

My stomach gave a nervous flip. I hadn't thought of that. "You're right, but I can't go home. By now both of my sisters will be there. If there's a killer after me, I can't endanger them."

"You're all . . . witches. Won't you be safer together?"

I considered his words. My sisters were formidable witches, but magic wouldn't stop a bullet, at least not the type of magic we practiced. "I can't go there. I won't put them in danger."

"Is there somewhere else you can go? Somewhere no one would expect you to be?"

I shivered, and not just from my soaking wet hair and clothes. There *was* somewhere no one would look for me. It had been months since I had last visited my mom, and she was remote. Few people in town even knew where she lived.

"I know a place. I'll be safe there."

He reached for the door handle. "Good, go there, and don't tell anyone where you are. I'll call you when I know more about Sasha."

"Hey Logan?" I said before he could step out.

He froze with the door halfway open.

"Thanks. I know in any other situation if someone were found with a hammer next to an unconscious woman, they would at least be taken in for questioning. Thanks for believing me."

He gave me a tight-lipped smile. "Adelaide, there are a lot of things about you that are hard to believe, you not being a murderer isn't one of them." He stepped out into the rain, leaving me alone with my thoughts.

And my dread.

I looked down at Spooky. "Over the river and through the woods we go, my friend. I hope you're ready, because I'm sure not."

He didn't have to speak into my mind for me to read the look in his eyes.

"Yeah, I know," I muttered. "Stop being a coward."

I started my car and pulled away from the street, heading east with my windshield wipers working furiously. Perfect weather for heading into the spooky forest . . . if you were in a horror movie.

CHAPTER NINETEEN

I called Luna on the way and told her what happened. Next, I called Evie and asked her if she could close up the cafe. Once those two things were done, I called my mom and told her I was coming.

"You should have been out here days ago," she lectured as my car slid on the muddy road.

I gripped the steering wheel white-knuckled with my free hand, making it through the puddle. I slowed and pulled off to the side of the road, barely able to see the trees through the pouring rain. "I may need you to come pick me up, I don't think my car can make it through the mud. I'm at the end of your road."

"Lock your doors and hang tight, dear," she said, her voice quickly transitioning from lecturing to caring mother.

"Thanks, mom." I hung up, lowering my phone as I

looked out through the rain.

The rain slowed down as I waited, allowing a thick mist to seep up around the trunks of the redwoods. Spooky stood with his paws braced against the door, looking out at the mist.

Goosebumps prickled up my arms beneath the sleeves of my damp coat. I glanced around, suddenly feeling uneasy with my headlights cutting across the trees. Not a single car drove in either direction on the road.

Spooky hopped in my lap just as I felt the dark magic coming near.

I slammed my hand down on the automatic lock switch, for what good it would do, and hunkered down in my seat, trying to look out all the windows at once. The narrow road to my mom's was nearly five miles long, it would take her a while to reach me with the mud. I was on my own.

The mist creeping up around the trees took on a green glow. I grabbed Spooky and clutched him to my chest. I shouldn't have braved the forest. I would have been better off driving around in the rain until Logan called.

My heart raced as I waited for whatever was coming. I jumped at a sudden light behind me, then I realized it was headlights, coming from the direction of town.

An old white truck pulled up beside my car. I knew I

had seen the truck around, but couldn't quite place it. The driver leaned across the passenger seat to roll down the window by hand.

I was trembling so badly, I fumbled pushing down the switch to roll down my window. Cold, wet air rushed into the car.

The truck's driver looked at me with concern. He was older, probably around my mom's age, with thinning gray hair and pale eyes. "Did you get stuck?"

Could he not see the green light seeping up through the mist? "M-my mom is on her way."

"I take it your mom is Imogene?" he asked. "Only a few of us live out here, and you've got hair like hers. I'm Ike, her nearest neighbor. I can give you a ride in that direction. She might've got herself stuck too."

I glanced back at the green mist edging toward the car, then down at Spooky in my lap. "You're Max's uncle?" I asked, wanting to confirm that this man wasn't a complete stranger.

His face lit up. "I wasn't aware he knew one of Imogene's daughters."

I forced a smile. The green mist was beginning to climb over the hood of my car. "I might just take you up on that ride. Do you mind if my cat comes?"

"Not at all. Should only take a few minutes to find your mom."

Holding Spooky tight, I grabbed my purse, unlocked

my door, then rushed over to his truck, flinging the door open before climbing inside.

Even though Ike was clearly a mundane with zero psychic ability, since he couldn't see the green mist, I still felt safer now that I wasn't alone.

He started driving slowly down the muddy road. He wore a pale blue fleece pullover, with only the edges of the sleeves wet, like he had been wearing a coat over it in the rain. "So how do you know Max?" he asked.

Oh, we just met when I decided to investigate your son's murder, I thought. What I said out loud was, "Sometimes he comes into my cafe. I own the Toasty Bean over on Main Street." I hesitated. "I heard about your son, I'm sorry."

He gave me a tight-lipped smile. "I'm afraid I always worried Neil would end up that way. He had a lot of enemies."

It seemed a strange way for a father to talk about his recently deceased son, but I didn't comment on it. Everyone grieved in their own way.

I glanced at him, trying to come up with a change of subject, and that was when I noticed his hands on the steering wheel. Underneath two of his nails was a line of dark red.

Spooky was looking at him too, but had issued no warning. Maybe Ike had just been painting. Or even cooking something like beets.

"It was kind of you to pay Neil's secretary," I said.

He kept his eyes on the road, slowly navigating the muddy ruts. "I covered a lot of Neil's debts over the years. I didn't hardly blink at one more."

"Sasha said you helped her too, she was very grateful."

His hands flexed on the wheel. "Neil took advantage of her most of all."

He started driving a little more slowly. I dared a glance at the backseat. There was a bundled up black, wet piece of clothing there. It could have been a hoodie.

Neil had been a huge financial burden on his father over the years. Ike had paid his debts and even helped Sasha save her house. Yet his truck was old and rusty, his clothes worn. Something told me he hadn't quite been able to afford all the help he gave.

Suddenly I remembered where I had seen his truck before. I had seen it at Desmond's. Ike had been driving to visit his son, and had seen me there with the homicide detective. Did Desmond know what his father had done? Had Ike worried that his son had just sold him out?

"The rain has almost let up," I said carefully. "I think I can walk from here."

Instead of stopping the truck, he turned off on a different narrow road, one that didn't lead to my mom's house.

I wrapped my arm around Spooky, prepared to run.

He pulled a small handgun out of the pocket of his fleece and aimed it at me. "I know you saw me at Sasha's, you can stop playing dumb. What, are you wearing a wire? Trying to get me to confess?"

Crap. Crap. Crap. My veins turned to ice at the sight of the gun. "If you had that all along, why didn't you use it on Neil and Sasha?"

He brandished the weapon. "Guns make murders easy to solve. Totally traceable. You have to understand, my son financially ruined me. And when Sasha found out what I'd done, she turned on me, even though I had done her a favor."

I edged my hand toward the door handle, wondering if I'd be able to open it quick enough to roll out.

He moved the gun, aiming it at my head. "Don't you dare."

My phone started buzzing in my back pocket.

"Don't answer that."

"So Neil took one too many loans from you," I breathed. "And you wanted him to stop taking advantage of Sasha. But what about Mary? I know she was somehow involved in all of this."

"The secretary?" he balked. "She was after Neil's money from the start, she just didn't realize that it was actually my money. She went after Desmond too, and was pretty bitter when he turned her down. But she didn't kill anyone."

While he was talking, I managed to get my hand on the door handle.

"Don't you dare—"

I threw the door open and rolled out as the truck went over a particularly large bump. I protected Spooky with my body, and we both toppled through the mud down the embankment.

With my breath ragged in my lungs, I stumbled to my feet and started running, nearly slipping as a bullet whizzed past my head.

Go left! Spooky shouted in my mind.

I darted to my left as another bullet sailed by, then I started running. "About time you chimed in," I rasped.

My boots slid in the mud, nearly toppling me every other step. I heard Ike's heavy footsteps behind me.

My heart leapt into my throat as the foggy trees ahead began to glow green. I had a killer behind me, and dark magic ahead.

Keep running, Spooky urged.

The fact that I was depending on the cat to keep me alive was so ridiculous, I might have laughed if my lungs weren't on fire from gulping down the cold air. I ran head on into the green glowing mist.

I knew it intended to kill me, but here was hoping it killed Ike first.

CHAPTER TWENTY

I panted shallowly, trying to keep my breathing quiet with my back against a massive redwood. Spooky pressed against my ankle, peering around the tree trunk. The mist was so thick I could barely see five feet in front of my face, and it all glowed a vibrant green. The feeling of dark magic was like bugs crawling over my skin.

The magic closed in. It whooshed into my lungs and filled my pores. I stifled a scream as it wrapped around my mind. It wasn't trying to kill me, it was trying to take me over!

It took every ounce of my will to keep the magic out of my thoughts. I noted distantly that Spooky was clawing at my leg, trying to warn me, but there was nothing I could do about it.

A hand clamped down on my shoulder. The cold

metal of a gun barrel pressed against my head. "End of the line, Ms. O'Shea."

I did the only thing I could think to do. I dropped my guard, letting the magic rush in. If it wanted to use me, that meant it at least wanted me alive. Ike did not. The power filled me up close to bursting, then settled into place.

"What the hell?" Ike's voice was suddenly unsure. The gun pulled away from my head.

My eyes snapped open, but it was like I was watching the forest on a movie screen. I wasn't the one in control of what I was looking at. My head turned, my eyes landing on Ike.

I wasn't sure what he saw in my expression, but his jaw went slack. He stumbled backward, the gun forgotten in his hand.

Spooky hissed at me as I started walking, but I ignored him. I stalked toward Ike. The dark magic pulsed through my veins, gathering in my hands. To my eyes, they glowed green, but I wasn't sure what Ike saw.

He staggered back until he hit a tree.

It was only as I lifted my hands that I realized I was about to kill him, and there was nothing I could do to stop it.

"Fight it, Addy!" my mom's voice cut across the forest.

"Drop the gun, Mr. Howard." Logan's voice, closer than my mom's had been.

I couldn't seem to take my eyes off of Ike. He dropped his gun into the mud and soggy pine needles, pressing his back against the tree. He raised his hands, palms out.

I closed the space between us.

I heard footsteps, then sensed my mom right beside me. "Fight it, Addy. You have to push it out."

My lip lifted into a snarl, my eyes still on Ike.

His breath came out in harsh pants. His body trembled. He sensed a predator before him.

I extended my glowing hands toward him, and his eyes rolled back in his head. He collapsed to the ground, unconscious, but the fight wasn't over.

"What's happening to her?" Logan hissed. Judging by the direction of his voice, he was right behind me.

"It's the same dark magic that was controlling Mr. Howard's ghost," my mom explained. "It has taken control of her."

I took one last look at Ike lying passed out on the ground, then turned my attention to my mom. Whatever was inside of me saw her only as a threat. My hands lifted. "Out of my way, witch."

She wore a long colorful dress, contrasting oddly with the foggy forest. She stepped fully in front of me, her hands down at her sides. "You won't hurt me, Adelaide."

Spooky ran past me toward her, pressing against her leg.

I gathered more magic into my hands. In my mind I was screaming, but I had no control.

I lifted my hands.

Addy, a voice whispered into my mind. *You are strong enough to fight it.* The voice wasn't Spooky, but felt somehow familiar.

"Ida," my mom gasped.

Let me in, Adelaide.

I could do nothing to control my body, but I still had some grasp on my mind. It was like opening a gate, letting the new spirit in.

The strangely familiar presence filled me, and suddenly I could breathe on my own, but just barely. The dark magic was still inside of me, trying to control me.

We will fight it together, but you must fight.

"I'll try," I rasped.

I wanted to reach out to my mom, but I was fighting for control of my hands. The dark magic wanted to use them to lash out, and I couldn't let it do that.

My mom seemed to understand my dilemma. She grabbed one glowing hand.

Spooky pressed against my leg.

It was like we all took a collective inhale, then we pushed the dark magic out. It went screaming through the forest, cast out, but not banished.

I collapsed to my knees, maintaining my grip on my mom's hand.

She knelt beside me. "Ida?"

Words that were not my own came out of my mouth, "I told you I should stick around."

She hugged me, and I wasn't sure if she was hugging her daughter, or her long-dead sister.

I sat there and let her hug me with Spooky rubbing his face against my extended hand. Maybe he felt like he was visiting Ida too.

Logan came into view as he moved toward Ike. He kicked Ike's gun away, then knelt to check the unconscious man's pulse.

I met Logan's eyes as he glanced my way.

He stared at me for a moment. "Are you . . . you again?"

"Kind of," I croaked. My mom pulled away so I could speak. "Ike killed Neil, and he tried to kill Sasha."

Logan took out a pair of handcuffs to put them on Ike. "I know, Sasha woke up and told me everything. Desmond had figured out what his father had done, and had confided in Sasha because they've been romantically involved. You didn't answer your phone, then Luna called me and told me you were in danger. She told me where to go. I met your mom on the road."

I was exhausted, but I managed a crooked smile. Luna's visions could be helpful after all. We had found the murderer, and had all come out alive.

There was still one issue though. I looked to my mom. "No offense, but I'd kind of like it if your sister's spirit would get out of me now."

My mom smirked. "She's right, Ida, it's time to go. We'll talk later."

I lifted my eyebrows. "So you knew your sister's spirit was hanging around all this time?"

"Why do you think I came back to live out here? This is where we grew up, she likes the woods. They help her hold on."

I thought for a moment I could hear Ida's spirit giggling like a little girl, then she left me. I slumped forward over my knees.

Logan moved to my other side, then he and my mom helped me stand. "Is this another one of those things I'm better off not understanding?" he asked.

I let out a weak laugh. "Definitely."

We all looked down at Ike as he struggled to sit up, but he couldn't quite make it with his hands cuffed behind his back. Spooky watched Ike like he was ready to attack.

"Did Desmond lie about arguing with Neil because of Sasha?" I asked.

Logan nodded. "The affair is what they were fighting about. Sasha didn't want anyone to know, so Desmond claimed he hadn't seen his brother."

So he had lied to the police to protect Sasha, and maybe himself. If it came out that they were dating, even with Neil and Sasha split up, it would have looked bad.

I glared at Ike. "You knew about the affair. You assumed Desmond would tell the truth and become a suspect, and that's why you tried to hit us with your truck. You were on your way over there to tell him not to talk."

Ike stared at his lap. "I want a lawyer."

I shook my head as another thought came to mind, the small turn of fate that had involved me to begin with. "At the very least you could tell me why Neil had my phone number in his pocket."

Ike glared up at me. "His latest scheme was to import coffee. He tried to blackmail me into funding the operation."

My jaw fell open. I had been drawn into a murder investigation simply because the dead man had wanted to sell me coffee. It was so silly it was almost funny.

Logan shrugged. "That makes sense, I suppose."

Scowling, I leaned heavily on my mom so Logan

could get Ike on his feet, then we slogged out of the forest together.

I was glad Desmond was innocent, but I had never expected Neil's murderer would be his own father. Poor Max. First he lost his cousin, and now his favorite uncle would be going to jail for a long time. He could lawyer up all he wanted. Now that we knew the facts, the case seemed pretty cut and dry. I would gladly testify against him, and after what he'd done to Sasha, I imagined she would too.

As far as I was concerned, he was getting off too easy. At least he didn't have a powerful dark magic trying to take over his body. Ida had helped me send it away, but it would be back. There might be few things in life I knew for sure, but that was one of them.

CHAPTER TWENTY-ONE

The next day Luna and I sat in my backyard while Spooky hunted bugs in the grass. It felt good to be home without an angry ghost coming after me, but I knew the dark magic could send another. The window repair people were supposedly on their way, but maybe I should tell them to hold off if it was just going to get broken again.

Even so, I felt pretty content as I sipped my coffee and leaned back in my lawn chair. I heard Callie's car pull up out front, then a moment later she came around the back of the house to find us. She opened the gate one-handed, lifting a little styrofoam cup of coffee in the other.

I raised an eyebrow at her as she came to stand before us. "If that's hospital coffee you need to go inside and get the good stuff."

Ignoring my advice, she relocated the third lawn chair, then sat forming a small triangle with us. "But it's so much better when you make it."

I rolled my eyes. If she thought I was getting up, she was crazy. After my near death experience in the woods, I was taking a day off—*of everything*. "How was Sasha?"

She leaned back in her seat. "They're keeping her one more day, but she should make a full recovery. Desmond was there."

I glanced at Luna, then back to Callie. "Did he say anything about his dad?"

She shrugged. "He avoided me, but he had brought Sasha flowers. After he left she told me they were finally going public with their relationship. She also said he was pretty torn up about his dad, but not entirely surprised."

My eyes widened. "Not surprised that his father killed his brother?"

"Ike had a lifetime of motivations building up. Neil trying to blackmail him when he refused to give him money was just the last straw." She sipped her coffee, then wrinkled her nose at the taste. "Have you talked to Max?"

I looked down at my cup. "Not yet. I figure I'll give him a few days to process the news."

"But aren't you two kind of dating?"

I let out a heavy sigh. "We were investigating a murder together. We haven't even been on a real date.

I'm not sure if he'll still want to take me out after all that's happened."

"Oh he will," Luna gave me a satisfied smile.

I narrowed my eyes at her, wondering if she'd had a vision about it. "Anything else you care to tell me?"

"Only that you'll be seeing more of the detective too." She winked at me.

I hunched my shoulders, not sure if that was a good thing or a bad thing. If he was smart, he would keep his distance from our strange little world. Even if Max and I continued dating, I planned to keep him out of it. For the time being, he could date Adelaide O'Shea, mundane. Maybe I would eventually tell him the truth, but only once I was sure things would stick.

I heard another car pull up on the street, and wouldn't have thought much of it if Luna hadn't stood at that exact moment. She looked down to Callie. "Let's go inside, I'll fix you a proper cup of coffee."

"But I want Addy to do it," she whined.

"*Now*, Callie."

Callie gave me a tortured look, but stood and followed Luna inside.

I wasn't surprised when Logan appeared outside the gate. "I hope you don't mind me coming back, I heard voices."

I forced a smile, unsure what he might have to say

after what he'd seen in the woods. "I don't mind at all, detective."

He opened the gate and stepped into my yard, glancing at Spooky still playing in the grass. "Sasha is going to make a full recovery," he said as he approached.

"I know." I raised my hands in surrender at his scornful look. "Callie visited her. I'm done sticking my nose into other people's business."

He took Luna's vacated seat beside me, gazing out across my overgrown grass. "Now why don't I fully believe you?"

"Because you're a cop and it's in your nature to be suspicious?"

He laughed. "I paid a visit to Mary this morning. I wanted to question her on a few things I had learned about her past. Once she heard Ike had been arrested, she came clean."

I sipped my cooling coffee. "Go on."

He lifted a brow. "What happened to staying out of other people's business?"

I rolled my eyes. "You can't just dangle that information in front of me and expect me not to be curious."

He grinned, then settled more comfortably into his seat. "Mary had left a bad marriage and was living under a fake name. She claimed the name change was to avoid her former husband, but it probably also had something to do with several counts of credit card fraud against her real name. She admitted she had come to Twilight Hollow with the intention of finding a rich husband."

"And that rich husband was supposed to be Neil?"

He laughed. "Not exactly. She learned early on that Neil had no money of his own, but by that point she was in love with him. After hearing Neil and Desmond's argument about Sasha, she actually thought Desmond had killed him."

I smirked. "So she's maybe a little bit criminal, but mostly just guilty of loving the wrong guy. I guess I can relate."

"To being a little bit criminal?"

I wrinkled my nose. "To picking the wrong guys."

"Like the veterinarian?"

I shifted uncomfortably in my seat. "None of your business, detective."

"Logan," he corrected.

I rolled my eyes. "None of your business, *Logan*."

We sat in silence for a moment, then he asked, "Are you safe?"

My spine stiffened. I definitely wasn't safe, but I wasn't sure if he should know that. "I'll be fine."

"But whatever that thing was, it possessed you. And it isn't gone?"

I frowned down at my coffee cup. "No, it isn't gone."

"And you're going to try to find it?"

I blinked at him. "What makes you say that?"

"This thing is after you. You don't seem like the type to take a passive stance."

He was right. We couldn't just wait around for the magic to gain strength and attack me again. "You shouldn't get involved."

"Who says I'm involved? I'm just curious."

I gave him a knowing look. "Liar."

He lifted his hands in surrender. "Okay, you win. Just promise me if things get too dangerous, you'll let me know."

I watched him for a moment, wondering why he cared. It wasn't like we had known each other for long. "If I think you can somehow help, I'll let you know."

He sighed. "That's fair enough, I suppose."

Callie and Luna emerged from the house, the latter carrying a tray with four fresh cups of coffee, one of which she handed to Logan. I set my last cup in the grass as she handed me a new one. Callie crossed her legs and sat in the grass, giving Luna the other free chair.

"So Detective," Luna began as she sat. "How does it feel to know that witches, magic, and ghosts are all real?"

Spooky abruptly hopped into his lap, leaving Logan to shake spilled coffee off his hand. After a moment of hesitation, he patted Spooky's head. "I think this cat might be the strangest part of it all."

Spooky purred in response, butting his head against Logan's fingers.

"Yes," Luna said thoughtfully, "I have a feeling there's a good reason he just came into Addy's life now, when he's been around all along."

Spooky stared at me from Logan's lap, as if trying to emphasize Luna's words.

I frowned, wishing he would just tell me why he had taken so long to come, but I seemed to only catch his words in bits and pieces.

After a drawn out silence, our conversation turned to more mundane matters. I leaned my head back, enjoying the sun on my cheeks. While I was curious about Spooky's motivations, the important thing was that he had come. I was a defective witch no longer. The dark magic had better watch its back, metaphorically speaking of course.

EPILOGUE

Two days later, I stood in my mom's spacious kitchen. I finished stirring the chocolate cake batter, then handed Callie the spoon to lick. On my other side, Luna mixed up the frosting.

According to my mom, chocolate cupcakes had been Ida's favorite, so we would be having some in her honor. I might just have to sneak out to the forest to leave a little offering for her, but not too far. No, I wouldn't be venturing into that forest alone again. I knew I'd have to face the dark magic eventually, but first I intended to learn just what it was, and what it wanted with me.

After I had poured the batter, Callie held the oven door open for me. "So, are you going to save a cupcake for your veterinarian friend?"

I scowled at her.

"Or perhaps the detective?" Luna said to my back as I shut the oven door.

I knelt to look at the cupcakes through the glass to hide my blush. Max was coming by the cafe in the morning to hear the full story of what had happened, minus the dark magic stuff, of course. And I'd be giving my official statement to Logan at the police station that afternoon.

Maybe I would save a cupcake for each of them. Heck, maybe I'd make cupcakes for the entire town. With an old dark magic to face, I might need all the help I could get.

NOTE FROM THE AUTHOR

Hello readers! I hope you enjoyed the first installment in Twilight Hollow. While this is the first book in my new pen name, Sara Christene, I have many other fantasy and paranormal series under my main name, Sara C. Roethle.

I do hope you'll take the time to check out my other books by visiting my site:

http://www.saracroethle.com

SNEAK PEEK AT CATNIP CANTRIPS
TWILIGHT HOLLOW BOOK TWO

"It's not out here," I groaned, well aware that my resistance was futile.

Luna marched down the hiking path ahead of me with redwoods looming tall on either side. We had a rare sunny day, and my sister was determined to use it.

Luna tossed her auburn braid over her shoulder as she glanced back at me. "That dark magic is out here somewhere. We can't just wait around for it to find you alone again."

"But is it really necessary to seek it out here?" Callie asked from behind me.

I looked down at my hiking boots as my sisters began to argue. Honestly, I was with Callie. I knew the dark magic would come for me again eventually, but confronting it out in the woods seemed like a bad idea.

There was no telling that to Luna though. She

wanted me to face my fears, so I zipped up my black down coat against the chilly morning air and kept walking.

"Meow," Spooky intoned at my side.

We all stopped and looked down at him, wondering if his meow was a warning.

Callie hugged her yellow parka tightly around her as her light brown eyes darted around the surrounding forest. "What's wrong with the cat?"

I watched Spooky sit down on the hard-packed mud, then he started licking one black paw.

"I think he's just tired. He hasn't given me any warnings since we've been out here." I pulled my cell phone out of my back pocket to check the time. "It's nearly eleven. I need to get to the cafe."

I lifted my phone in the air, searching for better service in case Evie had tried to get a hold of me. She was scheduled to work until one, but she had a young daughter. Sometimes things came up.

Callie looked over my shoulder at the phone. "Let's finish the loop, you'll get service back before the end."

I put my phone back in my pocket, then picked Spooky up to follow Luna further down the trail. We had chosen a hiking loop halfway between my mom's house and Twilight Hollow. It wasn't anywhere near the last places I had seen the dark magic, but we had already searched those areas high and low. My mom suspected the magic was rooted somewhere in the forest, we just had to find the right place and maybe we could figure out what it was and what it wanted.

I watched the surrounding woods as we walked, but nothing moved except for the occasional bird or squirrel. The right side of the trail began to taper off, gradually turning into a steep ledge. On our left the side of the mountain climbed upward.

I moved a little further from the edge, glancing down into the trees below, then stopped walking. There was something bright orange down there, maybe a jacket.

Not paying attention, Callie bumped into my shoulder. "Geez, warn me if you're going to stop in the middle of the trail." She tossed her strawberry blonde curls behind her back, searching for what has stopped me. Her eyes widened as she spotted the jacket. "Is that—"

Luna marched back toward us. "What are you two —" She spotted the bright orange. "Oh."

We all stared, because it wasn't just a jacket. There was a person inside of it, and judging by the bend in her neck, she was no longer amongst the living.

Callie moved a little closer to me. "Should one of us go down there? And by one of us, I mean one of you?"

I held Spooky close as a shiver marched up my spine. When I'd found Neil Howard just a couple weeks prior, I had expected that to be my last dead body for a while. "I don't think there's any helping her at this point." With one arm wrapped around Spooky, I pulled my cell phone back out of my pocket, then exhaled a sigh of relief. Two bars of service.

I selected Logan White from my contacts, then hit send before I realized what I was doing.

He answered on the second ring.

"You know," I said into the phone, "It must say something about you that you're the first person I call when I find a dead body."

"It says I'm a homicide detective," he answered. "What happened? Are you okay? Your sisters?"

Spooky started struggling, so I let him down to the ground. "Sorry, I should have led with that, we're all okay. We were just out on a hike, and it looks like someone fell off the trail. She's pretty far down so it's hard to tell how long she's been there."

"I'll call the paramedics. What trail are you on? Do you think you could send me a pin with the GPS on your phone?"

Glancing at each of my sister's haunted expressions, I explained where we were.

Through the phone I heard a rustling, then a car door shutting. "Send me the pin, and I'll make the call on the way. Just hang tight. If the victim is clearly deceased, there's no reason for you to go climbing down to her."

I stared at the body down the edge of the sharp incline. I wasn't sure I could make it down to her without breaking my neck too, so staying up on the trail seemed like a good idea. "Thanks Logan, we'll wait on the trail."

I hung up, then knelt beside Spooky as he peered over the edge.

"This was just an accident, right?" Callie asked to my back. "Like she slipped and fell off the trail?"

"Or she was pushed," Luna said. "There's no way of knowing."

"*Luna*," Callie hissed. "Don't say that. This is freaky enough as it is."

Luna shrugged. "We were all thinking it, don't blame me for saying it."

At a sudden thought, I straightened, then backed off the trail, further away from the drop. The trail was wide enough to fit two people side by side. The hiker wouldn't have needed to walk close to the edge if she had been on her own, and I didn't see anywhere that hinted the mud had given out beneath her feet.

I scanned the preserved footprints on the trail, but there were too many of them to make sense of, and they included several of ours.

I sighed. "If someone pushed her, we may have muddied up the evidence."

"Now is no time for puns, Adelaide." Callie said, though her eyes scanned the trail. "Let's just step back and try not to make any more footprints until Logan and the paramedics get here."

We all moved a little further off the trail, far back enough that we could no longer see the body down the incline.

With nothing left to do, I hugged my coat tightly around me and waited. I didn't want to think that someone had pushed the poor woman, but the idea plagued me. I also couldn't help but wonder if the dark magic had something to do with it. It had already sent one ghost after me. Here was hoping that it wouldn't send another.

ALSO BY SARA CHRISTENE

Tree of Ages

Tree of Ages

The Melted Sea

The Blood Forest

Queen of Wands

The Oaken Throne

Dawn of Magic: Forest of Embers

Dawn of Magic: Sea of Flames

Dawn of Magic: City of Ashes

The Moonstone Chronicles

The Witch of Shadowmarsh

Curse of the Akkeri

The Elven Apostate

Empire of Demons

The Duskhunter Saga

Reign of Night

Trick of Shadows

Blade of Darkness

The Will of Yggdrasil

Fated

Fallen

Fury

Found

Forged

The Thief's Apprentice Series

Clockwork Alchemist

Clocks and Daggers

Under Clock and Key

The Xoe Meyers Series

Xoe

Accidental Ashes

Broken Beasts

Demon Down

Forgotten Fires

Gone Ghost

Minor Magic

Minor Magics: The Demon Code

Printed in Great Britain
by Amazon